AIRSHIP 27 PRODUCTIONS

Comanche Blood
© 2017 R.A. Jones

Published by Airship 27 Productions
www.airship27.com
www.airship27hangar.com

Interior illustrations © 2017 Chris Kohler
Cover illustration © 2017 Adam Shaw

Editor: Ron Fortier
Associate Editor: Peg Livingston
Marketing and Promotions Manager: Michael Vance
Production and design by Rob Davis.

All rights reserved under International and Pan-American Copyright
Conventions. No part of this book may be reproduced in any manner without
permission in writing from the copyright holder, except by a reviewer, who
may quote brief passages in a review.

ISBN-10: 1-946183-06-7
ISBN-13: 978-1-946183-06-4

Printed in the United States of America

10 9 8 7 6 5 4 3 2 1

COMANCHE BLOOD

R.A. Jones

CHAPTER 1

"*Ride to the sound of the guns!*"

Those seven simple words had many times served as the rally cry of the Northern Brevet General George Armstrong Custer as he led his troops into battle during the Civil War.

Now, nearly a decade removed from that horrific conflict, in this early fall of the year 1874, those words still stirred the blood of Jason Mankiller as he heard the staccato sound of heavy gunfire coming from near at hand.

This lone drifter was nearly as distinctive in appearance as was the flamboyant "Boy General" under whom he had proudly served. A shade taller than six feet, Mankiller had the slender but muscular frame of a truly hard man. The thick black hair peeking out from beneath his flat-brimmed hat and his pronounced cheek bones spoke of the Indian blood carried down to him from his mother's side, though he possessed the pale, icy blue eyes of his father.

But what made him instantly stand out from other men was the distinctive *tattoo* that marked his left cheek. It ran from the corner of his eye halfway down the side of his face, in the shape of a teardrop. The ink was bright red.

A souvenir of sorts, meant as a badge of honor in recognition of his nigh-legendary heroics at the Battle of Gettysburg, the facial illustration inspired the name others gave him: one that was becoming increasingly well known.

The Man Who Cries Blood.

Some months earlier, he had stumbled into a new and lucrative new profession for which he seemed by both nature and talent to be ideally suited: that of the bounty hunter.

In that pursuit, he had quickly reaped a reputation for living up to his name: Mankiller. He tracked down only those who were wanted dead or alive by the law, and he took no great pains to bring outlaws in still in the latter condition.

The drifter had recently decided to take a short break from his deadly labors, making for the town of Fort Rogers, Texas, which he had decided to adopt as a home of sorts during such brief periods as he chose for respite from the trail.

But then had come the sound of the guns.

5

Drawing his Henry repeating rifle from its saddle scabbard, Mankiller urged his dun pony up the hogback ridge that rose before him, then reined in to survey the scene ahead of and below him.

No more than half a mile away sat a solitary stagecoach relay station. In front of it, stood an empty coach, engulfed in flames. One of the horses that had been drawing it, still tangled in its traces, lay dead on the ground. The other horses in the team were gone; as, apparently, were those that should have been in the vacant corral next to the depot building.

Circling the station was a score or more of Indians on horseback. Painted for war and whooping loudly, they were firing bullets and arrows at such a rate as to make it seem as though they had an inexhaustible supply of both.

Such was his knowledge of the various Plains tribes that Jason had no doubt they were members of some Comanche band.

Just two days earlier, he had skirted around a small Kiowa village to the north of this spot. Even though it was Kiowa blood that flowed in small traces through his own veins, even though he had spent time with them as both boy and man and was still known to many of them, he had seen no reason to risk being met with inhospitality.

These were bad days for the Indian, and hostility was running high and hot.

Even more so had he hoped to avoid contact with the Comanches. He was well aware that the name itself was not of their own devising, but rather had been derived from the Ute word for them: Ko-mants.

"Those Who Are Always Against Us."

There was great truth in this, for the Comanches treated almost everyone who was not one of them—Anglos, Mexicans, and other Indians—as an enemy. The one exception to this fatal worldview was the Kiowas, with whom the Comanches were allied.

These expert horsemen and fierce raiders of the Plains called themselves Nemernuh—"the People"—as though no others deserved to bear that appellation.

Those who feared the Comanches would be considered not cowardly, but wise.

One of the things that identified them to Mankiller as being Comanche was the total lack of any sort of headwear visible among them. Comanche men took great pride in their hair, which they wore long, braided and parted in the middle. The skin exposed by the part in their hair was often painted with red, yellow or white clay, and they preferred to wear no covering over their prized tresses.

Jason also knew that theirs was an empire greatly in decline, due to its decreasing numbers. Epidemics of smallpox and cholera, brought down upon them by the encroaching whites in the 1840s, had reduced their population from an estimated 20,000 to only a few thousand now.

Still, they were no less fearsome for their diminished numbers. The lean bounty hunter knew that the smart thing for him to do would be to simply ride around this battle that did not involve him personally.

Instead, he put the heels to his pony's flanks and sent it sliding down the hogback toward the besieged depot.

Though his rifle was now cocked and ready, he held his fire: it was virtually impossible to hit a target at any distance from the back of a galloping horse. Attempting to do so would be a futile and foolish waste of ammunition. Nor did the raiding Indians take notice of him, focused as their attention was on the stage depot.

As he drew closer to the encirclement, though, he brought the rifle up to his shoulder with one hand, taking careful aim. Seconds after he pulled the trigger, he was rewarded with the sight of a warrior pitching off his war pony.

Seeing this, three of the dead man's fellow Comanches reined up and turned their mounts in the direction from which the fatal shot had originated. They redirected their own fire toward this new intruder.

Keeping his horse's reins tightly clenched in his left hand, Mankiller twirled the rifle with his right, so as to ratchet the lever and slam a fresh round into the gun's chamber.

The three Indians seemed slightly taken aback by the fact that he continued to charge straight toward them, and their initial shots whizzed harmlessly around him. Even astride a bounding horse, the white man's aim was more accurate. His third shot roared straight through one of the Comanche's right eye, lifting him and flipping him back over the rump of his pony.

Jason's horse proved to be less lucky than he: he felt it shudder involuntarily under the impact of slugs punching into its heaving chest. Knowing what was sure to follow, the man kicked his feet free of the stirrups even while continuing to urge his mount onward.

The steed had heart, and carried its rider between and past the remaining two Comanches. It managed another fifty feet or so before its churning legs gave out under it and it pitched forward headfirst, flinging Jason forward out of the saddle. Even as he sailed through the air, he could hear the loud, dry snapping sound of the horse's neck breaking.

He landed on his feet, his knees absorbing the bulk of the jarring impact long enough for him to curl into a ball and roll onward. He came out of the roll on one knee, already snapping the rifle up to his shoulder.

Mankiller fought the instinctive urge to shoot the galloping Indian who was drawing closest to him. The second Indian, though farther away, already had his own rifle up and was drawing a bead on the kneeling white man.

Before this Comanche could pull his trigger, Jason sent a slug into his chest. The warrior dropped his weapon and slumped sideways off his mount.

Jason ducked and rolled, feeling more than hearing a bullet fired by the closest Comanche scream past him. The mounted warrior raced beyond him as he bounded to his feet.

The Comanche was pulling hard on the rein of his horse in an attempt to turn it when a bullet from the drifter's rifle slammed into his back. Before the pain of the wound could fully register in his brain, a shot fired from somewhere inside the stage depot took off the top of his head.

The Comanche's body had not yet hit the ground before Mankiller broke toward the station. He zigzagged slightly as his legs pumped furiously. Bullets began to whistle around him; one so close its high-pitched whine hurt his ears.

Then he saw a puff of dust kick up straight ahead of him—and realized that at least one of the defenders inside the depot building was shooting at him as well.

"I'm a white man, you damned fools!" he shouted. "Hold your fire!"

They must have heard him, for as he drew closer to the adobe building he saw its front door being flung open.

He didn't slow his pace by a step, literally hurling his body the final few feet through the open door and into a rolling tumble across the rough plank floor.

Before he could even fully rise to his feet and survey the scene, a virtual blur of satin and lace in female form practically bowled him over. The woman who had thrown herself upon him hugged him fiercely.

Befuddled, he pulled back away from her enough to look at her face—and was even more dumbfounded by what he saw.

"Jane?"

CHAPTER 2

"Thank God!" the woman gasped, staring up at him with fearful eyes and stroking his left cheek with one hand as if to assure herself that he was not merely a mirage conjured up by her terror. Her expression showed that Mankiller's mere presence had given her fresh hope of surviving this desperate ordeal.

His own lips curled in a tight smile as he stared back at her intently. Jane Starr was as strikingly beautiful as he remembered: statuesque and full-figured. Her hair, barely disheveled, was as black as was his own: her wide eyes also dark and mysterious. Full lips were opened slightly as she still sought to assure herself of the reality that he was amongst them.

"Decided to join the party, did you, Jason?" a male voice said, as a hand slapped him playfully on the back.

Mankiller turned to see yet another familiar face, one that showed its bearer was equally delighted to see him. It belonged to a man with the unlikely but true name of Cash Carpenter.

Ash-blond and coolly handsome, Carpenter was a professional gambler of the first order: originally from New Orleans. He and Jane traveled as a couple, both personally and professionally. While he plied his trade at the poker table, she usually ran a faro game. It was obvious that Cash had been as impeccably dressed as usual when he arrived at the station, though he had now removed his jacket, loosened his tie and rolled up the sleeves of his expensive white shirt.

"Your other guests don't seem too happy," Jason commented dryly.

"Nonsense," Cash replied in his soft Southern drawl. "They're the ones who started the festivities!"

"And how is it that you and Jane came to be here for this?"

"We've been traveling the circuit since last we saw you," Cash told him, speaking of the gambler's habit of meandering from town to town as the gods of luck dictated. There were at least a dozen such cities all gamblers hit on a regular basis.

"Our most recent route had taken us to Wichita, Denver and El Paso. Our last stop was Tascosa. We were finally on our way back home to Ft. Rogers when our aboriginal hosts decided to invite us to this little shivaree."

"Might I remind ya," a crusty voice interjected, "that them there so-called abo-whatsis is still out there—and still tryin' ta kill us?"

"Where are my manners?" Cash said. "My dear mother would be appalled by my lapse."

He motioned toward an older man squatting down beside a window. The man had hair and beard that were equally unkempt and equally gray.

"This gentleman is Walt Tungston," Cash explained. "The station master, and our host."

"We could still use a little he'p here, card sharp," Tungston said testily before turning and launching another shot out the window.

Carpenter laughed lightly and headed toward another of the station's windows. The fingers of his right hand were wrapped comfortably around the butt of the .38 caliber Navy Colt revolver he usually wore in the shoulder rig that could be clearly seen with his coat removed.

Only now did Mankiller take a few seconds to look about the rest of the depot. Near the back of the building, a lanky boy of no more than eighteen years glanced his way and gave him the bright grin of someone who clearly felt he was in the midst of a grand adventure. Standing beside a window on the east side of the depot was a stocky man wielding a double-barreled shotgun.

Jane took Jason by the arm and directed him toward the window she had vacated to greet him. A repeating rifle was leaned against the sill, and as she hefted it, the drifter raised an eyebrow.

"You any good with that?" he asked her, not in an unkindly fashion.

"Not very, I'm afraid," she admitted sheepishly. "I'm a lot better up close, with my pepperbox."

He knew she was referring to the .22 caliber "knuckle duster" hideaway gun the lady gambler kept secreted on her person while working.

"I'm not sure I've done any real damage at all yet," she confessed. "I can hit most any stationary target just fine, but it's entirely different trying to hit one that's moving."

Jason expected this was especially true since many of the Comanches rode with almost nothing of their body showing as they clung to the offside of their horses and fired from under the animals' necks.

"Aim for their horses," he directed her. "They're bigger targets, a lot easier to hit.

"You're still liable to kill or injure the rider if his horse goes down under 'im. And even if not, a man afoot will make a better target for you to hone in on."

She nodded that she would follow his directions, and poked the barrel of the rifle through the open window. He smiled grimly as she fired and he saw an Indian pony stagger, stumble and go down.

"Good girl," he told Jane. "We take out enough of their mounts and they just might decide that the price for taking this depot is stouter than what they're willin' to pay."

Himself being an excellent shot with either long gun or short, the bounty hunter focused on human targets. Such was his accuracy that every fourth shot or so brought the reward of seeing an attacker wounded or killed. It helped that he took his time, only squeezing the trigger when he saw the chance for a good shot.

From the outside, most of the lead being slung was harmlessly flattening against the thick adobe walls of the depot. The steady fire coming from all four sides of the station's interior effectively stopped the Comanches from tightening their circle and creating openings for warriors to attempt to enter the structure.

Approximately half an hour after Jason's arrival on the scene, riders began to peel away from the circle and head away from the station. The clouds of dust kicked up by their ponies' hooves briefly obscured them from sight.

When the dust cleared and settled, there was none of them in view: they had apparently galloped over and beyond a ridge a quarter mile south of the depot.

"Are they gone?" Jane asked hopefully.

"More likely they're just licking their wounds and planning their next move," Jason told her honestly. She tried to mask her disappointment by gamely levering a new round into her rifle.

"At least we don't have to worry about them starving us out," Jason said, peering out at the area in front of the depot.

"Why's that?" Jane asked.

He didn't look at her as he replied. "You done so much carnage with that there rifle of your'n—that we got plenty of horse to eat."

She responded by lightly bouncing her small handbag off his head. He turned to her now and grinned, and was rewarded by a returned smile.

CHAPTER 3

"Keep your eyes peeled, darlin'," Mankiller told Jane. "I'm gonna go parlay with the stationmaster." He raised up only partially as he moved away from the window.

"Mr. Tungston," he said as he approached the older man. "I didn't really get the chance to introduce myself earlier."

"No need to," the old-timer said. "Yer Jason Mankiller, ain'tcha?"

"You know me?"

"Know who ya are," Tungston replied. His left index finger traced a path from the corner of his eye down his cheek. "Yer sorta famous."

Jason grimaced slightly at the thought. "What's the situation here, Walt?"

"Bein' a relay station," Tungston replied, "we're pretty well supplied. Plenty o' grub. Fair amount of ammunition." He jerked his head in the direction of the man with the shotgun at the east window.

"That there's Sam Walthrop. He's the shotgun rider on the stage. Knows his beans." The station master turned his gaze toward the boy at the opposite window, who glanced in their direction at that moment and graced them with a wide smile and a wave as if he hadn't a care in the world.

"The boy's Homer Dean Smith," Tungston said. "My sister's oldest child." He lowered his voice and tapped his temple lightly with one finger.

"He's a little simple. But he's good people and a hard worker. He'll always do his best ta do whatever you tell him."

"It's obvious you already know the gambler. He's got sand. Same for his woman."

"Sure 'nuff," Jason said.

"That there's not so good," Tungston continued, pointing toward one corner at the back of the station.

In the blur of events surrounding his unplanned arrival on the scene, Mankiller had already spotted someone occupying that space but had not taken the time to look closely until now.

It was a middle-aged woman, seated on the floor beside a man who was stretched out flat upon it and partially covered by a blanket.

"The lady's name is Mildred Porter," Tungston told him. "Recently widowed, I gather. No kids to draw comfort from, so she's on her way back ta Indiana ta live with what kin she's still got livin'."

"The man she's tryin' ta tend to is Coop Martin, the coach driver. When the Comanch' jumped 'em a few miles west o' here, he took a bullet in the belly."

"Any hope for him?" Jason asked. Tungston shook his head.

"I figger he's a goner fer sure," the old-timer confided. "I ain't voiced that opinion to Miz Porter, though. The poor thing seems ta be a mite high-strung and fragile, and I don't wanna drive her inta hysterics.

"Lookin' after Coop keeps her from thinkin' about the trouble all the rest of us are in."

A nickering sound from the other back corner gave Mankiller the opportunity to voice the question that most baffled him. Standing there, surprisingly placid in the presence of so much activity and noise—was a pair of *horses*.

"You and Homer Dean always share your quarters with animals, do ya?" he asked Tungston dryly.

The grizzled stationmaster managed a chuckle as he shook his head. "No such of a thing! The boy was out in the corral, just startin' ta ready a fresh team of replacement horses for the stage, when the coach come a'thunderin' in to the yard.

"It was already on fire and the Comanch' was hot behind it.

"I done told ya the boy's simple. He kinda panicked and pulled them two horses along with him when he ran from the corral inta the station.

"He can be a stubborn little cuss sometimes—takes it from his momma, I reckon—so once he got 'em in here he downright refused ta turn 'em back out.

"Said he wasn't about ta let 'em be killed or captured by no red Indians."

Now it was Jason's turn to chuckle and shake his head.

"I'd best get back ta keepin' watch," Tungston declared. "I 'spect we ain't seen the last o' Mr. Lo." Jason recognized the epithet. Some Westerners used this in a mocking reference to the flowery descriptions of Indians made by some Eastern writers who insisted on romanticizing these native inhabitants of the frontier: as in, "Lo, the noble red man."

"I 'spect yer right, Walt," Mankiller concurred.

For himself, he chose to walk back and make his own assessment of the condition of the wounded stage driver. With little more than a glance,= he decided that Tungston was correct in both his assumptions: the man was about to die, and the woman was on the verge of a breakdown.

The driver was nigh on delirious with pain; his only conscious thought was in desperately trying to hold back his escaping innards with his own hands. A crude bandage was doing little to stop the seepage of blood from a second wound in his chest.

Mrs. Porter's eyes, as she looked up at Jason, were wide: the pupils dilated and almost unseeing.

The woman had simply been subjected to more burdens recently than her fevered brain could handle.

Jason bent, took her by the arms and, as gently as possible, lifted her to her feet. His face, which had brought fear to many a hard-bitten man, had no such effect on the widow, but rather seemed to calm her emotions.

"Why don't you let me tend to Mr. Martin there for awhile, Miz Porter?" he said softly.

"Oh, no," she practically moaned, pulling away from him slightly. "I couldn't do that."

"I got another job for you," Jason told her, "if you'll take it." Her gaze was still blank, but she ceased struggling against his grip.

"Do you think you could possibly brew us up a nice, big pot o' coffee? Mebbe you could even heat up some food if there's any already on the stove." He suspected there was; Tungston would likely have been preparing at least a light meal for the passengers to enjoy while their team was being changed out.

Mrs. Porter nodded stiffly. Such work as the drifter was suggesting had meaning for her: it represented a reality she far preferred to this one.

As she virtually stumbled away to begin her labors, Mankiller knelt down beside the mortally wounded Coop Martin.

In seconds, all of his senses confirmed what he suspected of the driver's condition. He smelled the distinctive, sour odor of the man's stomach contents spilling out of a perforated bowel: saw and heard dark blood bubbling out of nose and mouth from a punctured lung.

Martin had at most minutes to live.

The stricken driver's hand suddenly shot out and grabbed Jason's arm with surprising strength. He raised his head: his mouth opened and closed several times, but no words issued forth.

His head then dropped back hard against the floor as he expired.

Jason reverently positioned Martin's arms so they were folded over his chest, then pulled up the blanket partially covering him so that it went over the dead man's head. Mankiller stared down at the body for several minutes: his thoughts were for him alone to know.

The drifter at last rose to his feet and turned, nearly bumping into the widow Porter. She was standing before him with a steaming coffeepot held in one hand and a tin cup in the other. She seemed oblivious to the passing of the stage driver as she poured Jason a portion of the brew.

"This is mighty good, ma'am," he complimented her after taking a small sip.

Her eyes were still blank slates, but the corners of her mouth twisted as she attempted to smile. Unconsciously, she patted at her disheveled hair before scurrying away to see if any of the others in the depot desired coffee.

CHAPTER 4

Mankiller strolled across the room and took a seat on the floor next to Jane Starr, who was now also sipping at a cup of coffee. Moments later, the widow Porter approached them; she was carrying a bowl of stew in each hand.

"Care for something to eat?" she asked solicitously.

"I surely would, ma'am," Jason said eagerly, smiling up at her and accepting one of the steaming bowls.

"None for me, thanks," Jane demurred. The widow left the second bowl beside her anyway, before going to tend to the others in the station.

"How can you have such an appetite at a time like this?" Jane asked Jason, staring in amazement as he began to wolf down the contents of his bowl. "I'm not even sure I'll be able to keep this coffee down."

The drifter shrugged. "I've learned it's wise to take sustenance wherever and whenever I can, Jane," he explained to her, "'cause you never know when you'll get your next chance."

"Or *if*," she added grimly.

"I try not to ever think that way," he said philosophically.

"You really should try to get at least a little food in you," he urged. He set down his own empty bowl and resumed a kneeling position at the window, keeping watch.

From a spot where a bullet had cracked part of the widow sill, he extracted a thin splinter of wood and began to use it as a toothpick. Sparing a sideways glance, he smiled as he saw Jane pick up her bowl and take a small spoonful of thick stew into her mouth.

Mildred Porter, having served everyone, had retreated alone into a back corner of the depot. Sitting on the floor, she wrapped her arms around her knees, pulling them up to her bosom. Eyes closed, she began slowly rocking back and forth. Her lips moved slightly, soundlessly: perhaps mouthing the words of a prayer.

"We're gonna have to keep a close eye on her," Jason told Jane.

"Yes." Jane tilted her head back, staring up at the ceiling.

"I shot a man once," she said in a low voice.

"Oh?"

"He laid his hands on me."

"Then he deserved to be shot."

"I thought so. But I didn't kill him. I never killed anybody. Not till today."

Jason studied her face closely before he replied.

"You haven't killed anybody today, either, darlin'."

Her head snapped around to face him. "How can you be so sure of that?"

"I'm sure. All you took down today was a heap o' horse flesh."

"I'm glad," she sighed.

He simply nodded. He saw no reason to tell her that he believed at least one of her shots had indeed killed one of their attackers: he'd seen a warrior, peering out from under his horse's neck, have his jaw practically torn away by a slug that just missed the animal. If the shot alone hadn't killed him, the pounding hooves of the pony trampling the Comanche as he fell beneath it would have.

Mankiller's own heart was by now surrounded by a tough callus, grown thick by the number of deaths attributable to his actions. No need to inflict upon the woman's heart the wound such a deed could cause, he thought.

He could protect her from that, if nothing else.

"There's something I should tell you, Jason," she said softly. He turned his head to face her, saw that her own face was staring down into her bowl of stew, which she was stirring slowly with her spoon.

"Since the last time you saw me," she said in a confessional tone, "I wrote a book." She finally looked up at him, and he could see uncertainty in her eyes.

"It was a book about you."

He smiled reassuringly at her. "I know."

"You do?"

Jason jerked a thumb in the direction from which he had come to reach the station. "Somewhere out there," he told her, "in my saddlebags, is a well-worn copy of it."

The lady gambler who aspired to be a writer of thrilling penny dreadfuls looked stunned as he recited the lurid title of her first published dime novel book aloud:

The Life and Bloody Times of Jason Mankiller Texas Terror

-or-

Cowboy Cavalier

"Yessir," he chuckled, "you've become quite the slang-whanger, Janie girl."

Her face reddened brightly. "I had nothing to do with that title," she protested. "Swear to God, it was my publisher's doing, not mine."

"That's too bad," Jason replied with mock seriousness. "I was kinda flattered to think you saw me as a 'cowboy cavalier'."

"Oooh!" She buried her face in her hands, but then looked at him with a truly solemn expression.

"Are you mad at me?" she asked.

"What for?"

"Because I capitalized on your name to sell the book. Because I used knowledge I gained from you in private conversations without asking your permission.

"And mostly because I took the real you and twisted and exaggerated it and then put the new you into such melodramatic drivel." She had the look of the gravest sinner ever to face Saint Peter at the Pearly Gates.

"Have you really been carrying around so many worries with you?" Jason asked incredulously.

"I have," she replied. "And I've worried that if you found out, you'd no longer think of me as a friend."

He chuckled softly. "Well, just put them worries to bed, honeysuckle. Why, I'm plumb flattered that you chose to immortalize me in print. You do a man proud. And I tell ya: that there Mankiller fella you created is one ring-tailed wonder of a man."

"Oh, God," she groaned, covering her face to hide the blushing. "You hate him, don't you?"

"Hate him?" he repeated incredulously. Then he smiled at her. "Why, when I grow up—I wanna *be* him!"

"Oh!" She playfully swatted at him for teasing her.

"And don't you never belittle your talents, neither. Not in front o' me. You tell a crackin' good story, Janie—one I'll have you know I've already read and enjoyed three times!

"And as for the facts of the story…hell, you didn't stretch the blanket any farther than some of the other folks have who've told big windies about me over the years. To hear some of 'em tell it, I didn't even need the rest of the Union army to beat the Johnny Rebs!"

"You're not just being nice, are you?" she pressed. "I couldn't stand it if you thought I'd just played up to you for my own ends."

"I never thought that for a minute, Jane," he declared, reaching out and giving her hand a squeeze. "And I never will."

"That's good," she said, snickering rather abashedly and again covering her eyes with her hands for a second before casting a slightly wicked look his way. "Because I've already had a *second* Jason Mankiller dime novel published!"

He smiled broadly and shook his head as she attempted to project a look of innocence.

"I purely declare, woman, that if anyone's gonna make money off of my name—I'd like as not for it to be you." He leaned toward her.

"What's this one called?" he asked eagerly.

Now she was growing a bit excited. "The title is *Mankiller and the Curse of the Aztec Treasure –or– Death in the Desert.*"

He drew back, slapping one knee gleefully.

"I tell ya true enough," he said, "I've spent my share of time down Mexico way. When I've been there, I've found work, friends, the companionship of women, trouble," he gave her a wink, "sometimes on account o' the women—and dysentery.

"But I never found no treasure: cursed, blessed, or otherwise. Still, I look forward to reading whatever yarn you've spun around me. I truly do."

"Better hurry," she told him, "because I'm already at work on the third one!"

"Really?" he said. He was glad to see that talk of her literary endeavors had taken Jane's mind off the precariousness of their present position.

"Yes," she told him. "And my publisher is talking about having me come east and go on a book signing tour. He thinks that would boost sales even more."

"Hmm. I have to say, Jane, that I'm a little surprised you found enough audience interest to warrant more than *one* book about me. I'd guess the fact that you were asked to write more should serve as a tribute to your abilities as a writer."

"Oh, go on," Jane scoffed. "I think you're just underestimating the size of the appetite Eastern readers have for rip-roaring tales of the West—especially stories about men like you.

"I'll have you know, my publisher informed me that sales on our Mankiller books are eclipsed only by those dealing with such as Davy Crockett, Buffalo Bill Cody and Wild Bill Hickok!"

"The devil you say. I'll have to be sure to mention that fact to the two Bills, the next time I see 'em."

The woman giggled at his little joke—until she realized he wasn't joking. "You really do know Cody and Hickok, don't you?"

"Sure I do. I did a little buffalo hunting with Cody, and had a run-in or two with Hickok up in Kansas. He had a little trouble with some o' Custer's 7th Cavalry while I was scouting for the General."

Jane's mind drifted for just a moment, but then she smiled at him. "What a great idea," she enthused.

"What idea's that?"

"For my fourth book. A story with all three of you—together. It'll sell like lemonade at a 4th of July temperance meeting!"

The drifter looked at her admiringly. "You really like being a writer, don't you?"

"Oh, I love it, Jason," she said proudly. "If I keep doing well at it, I'd gladly give up my faro table." She smiled and winked at him. "But don't tell Cash I said that!"

"It'll be our secret," he promised. "And just so it's clear: you have my permission to keep writing stories about me from now till the cows come home, if that's what you want."

"Thank you." She used her hands to try to smooth down the blue dress she had worn for travel. "I've gotten some help with my efforts from another old acquaintance of yours, too."

"Who might that be?"

"Leslie Bellows."

"Ah." Jason remembered Bellows well, though it had been a few years since last their paths had crossed.

It had been Bellows, a highly successful newsman and photographer, who had been instrumental in creating and propagating the kind of outlandish stories that had made Mankiller a household name in certain circles. What Colonel George Wood Nichols had done for Wild Bill Hickok in his flowery articles for the *Harper's New Monthly* magazine, Bellows had done for Jason.

It was Bellows who had christened him "the Man Who Cries Blood" after the Battle of Gettysburg. Bellows who had filled the newspapers and magazines with distorted, virtually mythical tales of the heroic deeds of both Mankiller and the Boy General Custer: stories that had spread and become more outrageous with each retelling.

Bellows who was instrumental in branding Jason with his distinctive teardrop tattoo after the journalist helped get the young soldier drunk.

Yet, if pushed, Mankiller would have admitted he liked the rather unscrupulous rascal.

"And how is it Bellows helped you, Jane?" he asked.

"According to my publisher, Mr. Bellows helps promote my books by selling copies of them on consignment along with photos he took of you during the war. He carries them to the public appearances he makes all up and down the East Coast."

Jason remembered well Bellows penchant for taking photographs. After deciding Mankiller was a likely subject to be turned into a Herculean hero

"...you have my permission to keep writing ..."

of combat, the newsman had managed to snap nearly as many pictures of the former farm boy as he had of Custer and President Lincoln.

Nor did Jason doubt for a minute that the wily huckster was collecting a nice commission on all copies of Jane's books he sold, though he didn't voice that opinion to her.

"He's a real prince," he said instead.

"And I purely declare it's an honor to be an acquaintance of such a fine blue stocking as yourself." He saw Jane roll her eyes slightly.

"By God, it's true," he said. "Mark my word: you're well on the way to becoming the Queen of the Western Weeklies."

"You mean *King*," she corrected. "Remember—my readers all think I'm a man named 'Jay' Starr."

"That being the case," he speculated, "just how do you plan to pull off a book signing tour? I mean, much as it pains me to admit it, I have known a filly or two in my day who could pass for being a man in the right light," he declared, letting his eyes roam brazenly up and down Jane's figure, "but you sure as hell ain't one of 'em!"

Jane swatted lightly at him with one hand.

"My publisher thinks that by the time they've read my third book, they'll be willing to overlook that one flaw in my character."

"I know I would," he drawled slyly.

"Jason, you are—oh!"

Jane jumped as Mankiller snapped off two quick shots. He'd spied a Comanche scout trying to stealthily make his way in close to the depot. Too late, the Indian had learned such a plan was fatally flawed.

Jason cast his eyes about intently for sign of any other such infiltration, while Jane stared at him with equal intensity.

"Are we going to get out of this, Jason?" she said at last.

"I can practically guarantee it, darlin'," he replied without pause, hoping to project a bravado he didn't really feel.

"That's good," she said, choosing to take his word at face value and thus keep up her own courage.

"We'll have you back on your way in no time," he promised. "And one of these days you'll make it on to New York City. I know you told me you always wanted to see the place firsthand."

She seemed slightly surprised. "You remember that?"

"I remember purt near everything you ever told me, Jane," he declared, smiling softly.

It was at that moment that the Comanches chose to renew their assault on the depot.

CHAPTER 5

The fighting continued sporadically for the rest of the day, with the Comanches now content to feint and withdraw repeatedly, as if trying only to gradually wear down the depot's defenders both physically and mentally.

When the sun withdrew from the sky, so did they pull back: not leaving, but simply calling a halt to combat for a time.

As full darkness fell, Mankiller pulled Walt Tungston and the shotgun rider Sam Walthrop aside to hold a conference.

"I'd hoped that war party would lose interest," he said, "get wore out by the resistance, and be content with the damage they've done and the livestock they've managed to steal."

"I think we can fergit about that," Tungston spat.

"Yeah. But we can't just keep sitting here; we've got to do something, even if it's wrong."

"You got any ideas?" Walthrop asked. Mankiller was a stranger to him, but it was evident the drifter knew a thing or two about both Indians and fighting.

"Mebbe. First I have to ask you two: do you agree that the safety of your three passengers has to be the first priority?"

Both men grimly nodded.

"In that case, I have a plan that might at least allow them to escape. Of course, that would still leave us and Homer Dean behind to face whatever the Indians might have in mind."

"That's fine by me," Tungston avowed crustily. "But there's no reason for you to stay behind, mister. After all, you just had the misfortune o, stumblin' inta this situation. You don't work for the stage line; this ain't none o' yer responsibility."

Jason spared a glance at Jane, who was keeping vigilant guard at the window where she had stationed herself.

"I'm making it my responsibility," he told the other two men. "Besides, the two horses we have are gonna be asked to carry three people outta here as it is; they couldn't bear up under a fourth." He put a hand on Tungston's shoulder.

"I'm just sorry that means poor Homer Dean will have to stay behind, too."

"That is a shame," the stationmaster agreed, looking over at his nephew.

"But it can't be helped. My sister Emma would understand."

The men waited till well after midnight before beginning to implement Jason's plan, in hopes the Comanches besieging them would be sleepier and less vigilant then.

At the direction of the bounty hunter, Jane Starr and Mrs. Porter had removed their dresses and exchanged them for pants and shirts belonging to the slightly built Homer Dean.

"It's time," Mankiller said at last. "Cash, you and the women follow me." He hadn't yet shared the details of his desperate ploy with the three of them, but all followed him without objection.

Jason led them to the back of the depot, where the two horses Homer Dean had rescued were tethered. Each animal wore a rope halter but no saddle: Jason had tossed a blanket over the backs of both.

"Up you go," he told Cash, pointing to the farther of the two mounts. The gambler cocked an eyebrow quizzically but did as he was directed, nimbly hopping up on the beast.

Mankiller then hefted Mrs. Porter off her feet and virtually slung her up onto the second horse; the woman offered no resistance, as by now she was in a nearly catatonic state. Jason then far more gently assisted Jane up to sit behind the older woman.

"Listen up," the bounty hunter said, directing his words at the card sharp. "You need to do exactly what I tell you, Cash."

"I'm yours to command," his friend replied, smiling thinly and giving him a careless salute.

Jason nodded. "Keep an ear out. In a little while, you should hear gunfire coming from the west. When you do, wait a minute, then lead the women outta here, moving to the northeast.

"Wait till you're at least a mile away from here, then cut back south to the main stage road. Once you find it, follow it due east.

"Don't bother to try anything fancy like backtracking or covering your trail. Just ride as fast as the conditions will safely allow.

"Don't look back and don't stop for anything, save to rest the horses as they need it, until you reach the next station or settlement. Can you do that?"

"Yes," was all Cash said: though he was clearly not happy with this plan of escape, he saw the wisdom of it.

Hearing this exchange and knowing what it likely meant for those who remained behind, Jane pushed herself back and slid over the rump of her horse and rushed to Jason's side.

"I won't do it," she huffed desperately. "I won't run away and just leave you behind."

"You have to, Jane," he said firmly. "There's no other way. Miz Porter is incapable of taking care of herself. You have to go with her."

"Cash could –"

"No," he snapped. "Everything will be all right, darlin'. I promise. In a few days, I'll meet back with the two of you in Ft. Rogers. We'll all have a drink to celebrate."

They both knew he was whistling in the dark, but Jane bravely smiled and nodded and allowed him to put his hands around her slender waist and again lift her up onto her horse.

"Look at it this way," he said with feigned cheerfulness. "If nothing else, all this'll give you another good yarn to write about."

"It just better be one that has a happy ending," she said firmly.

"It will be," he told her. Then his face took on a more serious demeanor.

"That little pepperbox pistol you mentioned earlier," he said. "Do you have it on you?"

"Right here," she replied, patting at a bulge in her right pants pocket.

"If they come after you," he said haltingly, "if it looks like you're gonna fall into their hands…"

"I know, Jason," the lady gambler finished for him. "One bullet for Mrs. Porter…and the next one for me."

Mankiller nodded grimly, gave her hand a gentle squeeze, then turned his back and walked away from her.

CHAPTER 6

"I want you to keep a sharp eye out for me, Walt," Jason said as he took up a position near the front door of the depot. "If I make it back—I don't wanna get shot by one of my own."

The aging stationmaster nodded his understanding.

Mankiller leaned his rifle against the wall, fearing it might hinder his movements once he stepped outside.

He signaled with a jerk of his head and Tungston yanked open the door. All lights within the depot had been extinguished so as not to send an illumined warning to any who might be watching. The bounty hunter bolted through the portal and the old-timer quickly and quietly closed it behind him.

Jason scurried crab-like toward the partially burnt shell of the nearby stagecoach; the flames had petered out before completely consuming it. He chose to take encouragement from the fact that his movements had thus far drawn no fire from the Comanches.

Remaining crouched low to the ground, he raced westward away from the coach. About fifty yards from the relay station, he came upon a shallow gully. Cautiously peering over its near edge and seeing no one, he slid down the slope and clambered up and over the opposite rim. Flat to the ground, he began to crawl slowly southward.

A faint sound coming from ahead caused him to stop. Raising his head slightly, he saw a dark figure about twenty feet away. It was an Indian, a blanket wrapped around his shoulders, sitting on the rim of the gully. Clearly a lookout, he was facing in the general direction of the stage depot. Either because of the distance or the weariness of his eyes, the sentry had obviously not spotted Jason leaving the station.

Turning his body slowly and silently, Mankiller crept away from the edge of the gully for a ways, then angled back toward it in a manner that brought him back directly behind this lone guard.

Even before he reached that spot, the lone drifter had pulled the razor sharp skinning knife he carried on his belt. Rising to his knees, he clamped his free hand over the Comanche's mouth to stifle any outcry and dragged him back away from the gully's rim.

With deadly efficiency, he slit the sentry's throat with the skinning knife. He whipped his right leg over those of the Comanche to suppress the thrashing that convulsed the Indian's body until he bled out.

Wiping the blood off his hands and blade with the dead Comanche's breechcloth, Mankiller slithered back to the edge of the gully and looked over it. Below him, he saw three more Indians stretched out on the ground, seemingly asleep.

Feet first, he carefully slid down the side of the gully, moving then to stand over the slumbering Comanches. None had stirred, so silent had been his killing of the sentry and his descent to where they lay.

Now came the truly dangerous part. The bounty hunter's scheme was to draw the Indians' attention away from the relay station long enough for Jane and the others to get a head start in escaping. But for that plan to succeed, Mankiller now needed to make plenty of noise.

He drew his pistol and took careful aim at the nearest sleeping Comanche.

Back inside the depot, Jane Starr's body jerked reflexively as she heard three shots and a loud war whoop ring out in the night.

Walt Tungston stood nearby, staring down at the face of his pocket watch, precisely counting down the seconds as Mankiller had directed him. More shots had begun to pop off to the west by the time the required sixty seconds had elapsed.

"Get movin'!" he shouted, swinging open the back door of the depot and motioning with one arm.

"Yaaah!" Cash urged his mount. The horse fairly leapt through the door, the second steed hard on its heels.

As they galloped away, Jane managed to take one last glance over her shoulder, looking back in the direction where she knew Jason was now fighting for his life. Fighting for her life.

The one glance was all she could spare, as all her attention was needed to guide her racing mount. She had to do it all, for the widow Porter was by now practically dead weight and of no real use at all.

Back in the depot, the minutes seemed to grind by with agonizing slowness. All three of the remaining men had now taken up positions at the front windows, keeping close watch. Occasionally they saw flashes of light punctuate the darkness, accompanied by the crack of a gunshot. Just as their nerves became taut as bowstrings, they spotted a shadowy figure racing toward the depot. They assumed this to be the bounty hunter, for he was being pursued by several other howling figures.

Sam Walthrop and Homer Dean opened fire, taking care to send their shots well away from the lead figure rapidly drawing near.

Waiting until the last possible instant, Walt Tungston at last flung open the front door of the depot, in time to see Jason Mankiller dive through and roll across the floor.

Just as quickly, the stationmaster tried to slam the door shut, only to be pushed back as a burly Comanche plowed into it with one shoulder.

Mankiller had ended his tumble by rising to one knee and rapidly snapped off two shots. The third time he squeezed the trigger, the hammer came down on an empty chamber.

Luckily, the first two shots had done the job. The Comanche was still upright, but his eyes had gone dead as twin patches of blood bubbled out of his chest. Tungston shoved him out of the doorway and banged the portal closed, barring it locked.

The withering fire Sam Walthrop and Homer Dean continued to lay down drove the remaining attackers back until they disappeared into the darkness.

Walt Tungston moved to Jason's side, reaching out to take his left arm and help him rise from the floor. Only then did he notice that the shirtsleeve covering that arm was stained with blood.

"How bad they getcha?" the stationmaster asked.

"It's just a scratch," Mankiller insisted, pulling his arm away so as to use the left hand in assisting with the reloading of his pistol.

"What about Cash and the women?"

"They took off outta here just like you planned," Tungston told him. "And subsequent, I didn't hear no gunfire comin' from that direction."

"I hope that means they got away," Jason sighed in relief.

"Mebbe they'll be able ta send us some help," Homer Dean offered, grinning innocently.

"Sure they will, boy," his uncle replied.

But the look the stationmaster exchanged with Mankiller revealed they both knew there wouldn't be time for any help to arrive.

CHAPTER 7

The rest of the night passed fairly uneventfully, with the Comanches only sending an occasional bullet the depot defenders' way, to let them know that they were still boxed in and to insure that the whites couldn't relax their guard long enough to sleep.

The gray skies had barely begun to give way to the pink of dawn when the Indians again launched an all-out assault on the station, this time coming in from all sides on foot.

"Make every shot count, boys," Mankiller counseled, taking aim with his rifle.

He found his own aim to be hampered by the number of shots coming his way from outside, scorching the air and splintering the wood of the windowsill around him.

A sickening, wet splat and pained gurgling snapped his head to one side in time to see Walt Tungston stagger away from his post. The stationmaster's hands grasped at his throat, from which blood was spraying darkly. He pitched over backwards.

"Uncle Walt!" Homer Dean cried out in a strangled voice, rushing to kneel beside the prone Tungston.

Mankiller snapped off three shots in rapid succession, then raced over to where Homer Dean knelt next to his uncle's unmoving form. Jason grabbed the boy by the back of his shirt collar and yanked him roughly to his feet.

"He's dead, son," he told Homer Dean, ignoring the tears streaming down the simple boy's cheeks. "Get back to the window and commence to shootin'!"

He gave the grieving boy a light shove; saw him retrieve his rifle and resume firing. Mankiller returned to his own post and noted their attackers were drawing inexorably closer.

Above the general din of the battle and the deafening shots of his own rifle, the drifter heard a new and disturbing noise.

It was coming from above, from the roof of the station.

His first thought was that the Comanches had begun to drop flaming arrows down on the depot, in an effort to either smoke out the white men inside or burn them alive.

But then he realized the sound was that of men moving around up there. The banging noise that soon commenced told him they were attempting to hack a hole in the building's wood shingle roof.

So many of their fellow warriors were still rushing the station from ground level that the bounty hunter had no choice but to ignore the danger from above. The barrel of his rifle was growing hot in his hand as he pumped rapid fire into the charging Comanches.

At last, a bullet whistling dangerously close past his head from behind left him with no choice but to turn away from the window. He spun to see a painted warrior peering through what was now a hole in the roof large enough to accommodate an average sized man; the Comanche was taking aim for a second shot at Mankiller.

The bounty hunter was quicker. With the butt of his rifle braced against his hip, he fired upward. His Comanche target dropped his own weapon and plunged through the hole in the roof. He struck the floor below headfirst and lay with his neck twisted at a gruesome angle.

"Walthrop!" Mankiller yelled at the shotgun rider. "They're comin' in through the roof!"

Walthrop leaped to his feet, turning in time to see two attackers trying to push their way through the gap in the ceiling at the same time. The white man threw his shotgun to his shoulder and tripped both triggers.

The resulting spray of buckshot caught both of the Comanches with deadly, shredding consequences. Their limp bodies momentarily blocked the opening in the roof. Walthrop broke open his shotgun, pulling out the smoking shells and replacing them with fresh ones.

Before he could make another move, several shots lanced through the window behind him, striking him in the back. His body was flung forward, flopping face down on the rough floor.

Mankiller's eyes narrowed as he saw the shotgun rider go down. The attackers on the roof had already managed to clear their fallen comrades away from the hole, and one of them now dropped down into the depot.

Standing over Walthrop's body, the warrior pumped another bullet into the man's back. Dropping his rifle, the Indian knelt down astraddle the dead man. Yanking Walthrop's head back by the hair, the Comanche pulled a knife from his belt, preparing to take the shotgun rider's scalp.

A bullet from Mankiller's rifle slapped into the Indian's forehead, lifting him and throwing him off Walthrop.

A new source of imminent danger presented itself as Jason turned back to the window. Several attackers had reached the front door and he could hear shoulders furiously pounding against it. He knew it would not be able to withstand this for long.

Such was the angle that he could not get a clear shot at any of them, so instead he resumed lacing lead at others rushing the station.

When he expended the last of the rounds in his rifle, he cast the weapon aside: he knew he wouldn't have time to reload.

Reaching across his belly as he rose to his feet, he drew his pistol from its cross-draw holster and backed toward the middle of the room. He turned briefly to send a couple of slugs through the hole in the roof and keep those attackers off balance.

The wooden bar holding the front door cracked and then shattered: Indians poured into the depot.

Standing sideways to them, Mankiller placed his remaining four shots with fatal precision. He then dropped the useless weapon and pulled his skinning knife.

A great weight hit him from above as a Comanche warrior dropped down from the roof. Those who his gun had held momentarily at bay now rushed forward and swarmed over the drifter.

Even as he tried to defend himself, Jason saw several more attackers had young Homer Dean pinned to the wall. The poor, simple boy was weeping and screeching pitiably even as war axes and knives were horribly hacking him down.

Mankiller gave a better account of himself, using his knife to slash and rend; but sooner rather than later he was dragged down to the floor by sheer weight of numbers. Pain exploded in his head as a hatchet blade slammed against it in a glancing blow. Whoops of bloodlust assailed his ears.

Above that noise, a loud, guttural command rang out in Comanche. It was a tongue with which Jason was somewhat conversant: picked up during the times he spent as a boy with that tribe's allies, his grandmother's people the Kiowas. At this shouted order, the fighting ceased.

Mankiller was still alive, though severely battered and bleeding from multiple lacerations. Strong hands painfully pulled his arms back behind him and forced him up onto his knees.

The Indians gathered in front of him parted ranks to make way for the warrior who had shouted out the command: the man Jason assumed to be the leader of this particular war party.

He was a cruel-faced man with angry, almost evil eyes. His mouth was little more than a thin slash across his jaw. A horizontal stripe of white paint ran across his forehead; intersecting it was a red stripe running vertically down the middle of a broad, flat nose.

Jason had always thought of the Comanches in general as being a mighty handsome people: this man was the exception.

The bounty hunter's eyes danced in barely disguised surprise, as he next saw three *non-Indians* stride into the depot close on the heels of the cold-eyed Comanche leader.

One had the look of a half-breed, the next a Mexican and the third an Anglo. The Mexican had both hands full carrying the scorched strong box he had doubtless retrieved from the burnt-out stagecoach.

Mankiller thought it likely that the three also intended to rob the dead of any money and valuables they might have on their persons, while leaving the Comanches to filch weapons and anything else that might strike their savage fancy. He had heard of such men as these, who consorted and conspired with the Indians.

They were known as *Comancheros*—and he had no doubt that these three men were of that despicable breed.

These brigands roamed freely and widely throughout New Mexico and West Texas. Initially, they mostly traded such items as cloth, beads, coffee and steel arrowheads to the Indians in exchange for mules, horses and hides. Sometimes they would barter for Indian slaves and essentially sell them to landowners in New Mexico for cheap labor.

Later, they started dealing for captive Mexicans and Anglos that they could then return to their families in exchange for ransom money.

Some were darkly rumored to have begun trading liquor and firearms to the Indians. They often took rustled cattle in trade, selling them then to merchants and government beef contractors.

Unknown to him, the three Comancheros who now faced Jason had recently traded a handful of rifles to this band of Comanches, who in return offered their help in attacking the stage depot.

The Anglo appeared to be the leader of this trio of renegades, and he now conferred in low tones with the head Indian.

"Lookee here," the half-breed said in mocking tones, stepping closer to Jason. "This fancy boy's so scared he's *cryin'*!"

Mankiller ignored the sarcastic reference to his tattoo and made no reply. He chose instead to use what time he had studying the faces of the three Comancheros. He wanted to remember them clearly, for he fully intended to meet them again when he was not at such a hopeless disadvantage.

The breed appeared to be part Apache, though from head to toe he affected the garb of a Mexican *vaquero*. The true Mexican wore only a sombrero that reflected his blood heritage: otherwise, he was dressed in buckskins. The look of him led Jason to suspect he had been a *cibolero*: a New Mexican buffalo hunter. Both his thick moustache and his eyes seemed to droop sadly.

The Anglo with them was thinner but taller than the other two. He wore a dirty leather patch over his left eye and was missing the little finger of his left hand. He sneered as he stepped away from the Comanche leader and moved nearer to the captive bounty hunter.

"He'll be doin' more than cryin' when our friends here get done with him," the Comanchero declared coldly. Mankiller met his gaze without flinching.

"Did you talk that bold to the woman who plucked your eye out?"

The Anglo's ugly face grew even uglier with anger and he reared back the rifle he had gripped in his hands.

The last thing Jason saw before the darkness descended upon him was the butt of the weapon headed straight for his face.

CHAPTER 8

Mankiller awakened to excruciating pain.

From the shadow he cast he knew the sun's position marked the passing of some hours since he had been taken captive.

Once consciousness returned, the fog clouding his brain quickly dissipated and he was able to take stock of his situation.

He was no longer inside the depot but out of doors. The source of his pain came from the manner in which he was tied up. His arms had been lashed to a long lodge pole, which in turn was suspended across and between the branches of two trees at such a height that his feet did not touch the ground.

Gravity's pull upon him caused lances of agony to shoot through his shoulders, back and chest. His head pounded from the rifle blow it had taken. Every cut and bruise he had sustained seemed to beat with its own discomforting rhythm. He had been stripped of all his clothes.

The Comanches had left him strung up like a butchered steer a short distance outside their village. Perhaps a hundred yards away he saw the large circle of their tipis. It was no small encampment, numbering perhaps as many as fifty or sixty lodges.

Drifting on the wind came the sounds of plaintive wailing: the cries of women who had lost husbands, brothers and sons in the raid on the stage depot.

Jason had instinctively flexed his arms to raise his body and relieve some of the painful pressure squeezing at his heart and lungs. Having held that position as long as he could, he now sagged downward. As he did, he lowered his head—and found himself looking into the eyes of a small boy.

Those dark eyes widened and the child drew one arm back. He was holding a rock the size of his fist, and now flung it at the white captive as hard as he could. Mankiller grunted as the stone banged off his left ribcage.

The boy ran a short distance away and began to yell at the top of his lungs. In response, other children and those women of the village not engaged in mourning rituals came running.

As was the custom of the tribe, the boys under the age of about nine were naked; even the girls who had not yet reached puberty were dressed only in breech cloths. But they all came bearing sticks and stones, and along with the women proceeded to make use of them.

Jason twisted right and left as much as his bindings would allow, but most of the thrown stones hit their mark. The braver among his tormentors rushed in close enough to whack him sharply with sticks.

The boy who had pelted him with the first rock, like a warrior counting coup now darted forward and delivered a vicious kick up between Mankiller's legs and into his groin.

Jason's body involuntarily lurched upward, his lungs sucking in air. As he dropped back, his weight caused the lodge pole to which he was lashed to bow; though not quite enough for his feet to touch the ground.

His tormentors laughed at his obvious pain and resumed pummeling him. The edge of a hurled stone struck him at his hairline, lacerating the scalp and sending blood cascading down into his eyes, the right one of which was beginning to swell shut.

The trussed up drifter was beginning to think he should have followed the advice he gave Jane, and saved a bullet for himself.

But the greater part of him was still thinking of escape.

A woman called out an alert as she spied several of the men now approaching from the village. She and the other women and children now deserted their torture, backing away several paces.

Mankiller recognized the warrior at the forefront as being the man who had led the raid on the stage depot. The bounty hunter cast his eyes about, but saw no sign of the three Comancheros.

As the Comanche leader drew close, Jason got an even closer look at him than he had at the relay station. As did many other men of his tribe, this one wore a single, slender scalplock of braided hair, decorated with beads and a single feather, which hung down over the right side of his face.

Both his ears were pierced, with silver hoops dangling from the lobes. Tattoos of various shapes and colors decorated his bare chest. In contrast to him and the other men, the women of the village gathered about wore their hair short, though they equally enjoyed painting themselves. They seemed to be especially fond of red and yellow circles around their eyes.

Jason also noticed that this taciturn warrior now wore the bounty hunter's gunbelt, with his pistol in the holster, his skinning knife in its sheath. The Indian also carried a small quirt, with several rawhide strands and a loop that went around his wrist.

As he drew even nearer to the captive, the Comanche pulled out the skinning knife. He began to use it expertly, slicing off thin slivers of flesh from Jason's chest and arms.

Mankiller knew they wanted to hear him scream. He also knew that sooner or later he would do so. No man—white or red—could silently endure endless pain. But the drifter meant to deny them that pleasure for as long as possible: clenching his teeth tightly to choke back any such cries.

Even more men came to watch the spectacle, and the Indian leader sheathed the knife for the moment. With an audience gathered, he began to strut proudly back and forth in front of the helpless captive.

"Listen to Wolf Track," he blustered, "and look at the white man hanging like a rabbit being dressed for the stew pot.

"The others of his kind weren't so lucky. They didn't fight as well as our babies could." Several of the other men grunted their approval.

"With me leading the way," Wolf Track boasted, "we killed them all, took their scalps, stole their horses and burned their lodge to the ground.

"With my own hands I killed at least three of them, after counting coup. I only wish there had been more of them, so I could have—"

"Wolf Track!" another man abruptly interrupted. He pointed to the captive white man, whose body was hanging limply now from the lodge pole.

"I think he's *dead*!"

CHAPTER 9

Two of the Comanches cautiously approached the captive white man, whose unmoving head had dropped down to his chest.

The warriors tensed as Jason suddenly emitted a loud and raspy snoring sound.

"He's not dead," one of the men cried out in amazement. "He's *asleep*!"

The man grabbed the captive's hair and yanked his head up. Mankiller, who had only been feigning slumber, now pretended to be awakening.

"I'm sorry," he said, further surprising the onlookers by addressing them in their own tongue, "but that big horse's butt lies so poorly that he put me to sleep!"

Hearing this, several of the gathered warriors began to laugh and hoot, mocking Wolf Track.

The shamed warrior let out a cry of rage and leapt forward. Men stumbled back out of his path as he began to flail wildly at Jason with the lashes of his rawhide quirt.

Unintelligible noises issued up from his chest as he struck again and again. Jason's body danced horribly as it became laced with red welts; some so deep they quickly began to ooze blood.

None sought to halt the lashing, nor would Wolf Track have stopped himself had not the sounds of a slight commotion in the village not reached his ears and penetrated the killing haze that clouded his mind.

Another small band of warriors had entered the encampment, led by a tall man on a large gray pony.

This tall man swung both legs over the right side of his mount and dropped gracefully to the ground. As he did, a slender woman (his wife) approached and began to talk to him. She appeared rather animated, occasionally punctuating her words by pointing toward the crowd gathered around the captive white man.

Placing his hands lightly on her shoulders, the tall man addressed the woman, who nodded before scurrying away.

Those gathered around Jason again parted deferentially as the tall warrior strode over to join them. He was a man of striking good looks, with an aquiline nose and light gray eyes that spoke of a mixed racial heritage. Around his throat he wore a necklace that prominently displayed a single claw from a bear, the animal that was his spirit guide.

"You're just in time," Wolf Track informed the new arrival, "to join in the sport!

"Best hurry, though," he crowed. "I haven't left much of him for you!"

The tall man did not grace him with so much as a single word in reply, walking straight toward the captive, whose head was now slumped down on his chest for real. The Comanche took hold of Jason's hair and lifted his head.

An audible intake of air escaped from the warrior's mouth as he spied the distinctive teardrop tattoo on the white man's left cheek.

Mankiller looked squarely at the Comanche, using the one eye he had that wasn't swollen nearly shut and smiled at him with cracked and bleeding lips.

"Hello, *Quanah*."

CHAPTER 10

The gray-eyed Indian named Quanah released Mankiller's hair as if its touch had burned him to the bone, spinning away from the captive.

"Do you know who you've brought into our midst?" he angrily demanded of Wolf Track.

"This is the man whose tears are blood!" he exclaimed, pointing to the tattoo on Jason's cheek.

Anxious gasps and murmurs rose from those gathered around. All of them knew of this man, or at least had heard furtive tales of him. He was known to be part Kiowa, and to be called by them *"Kills Many."* In his youth he had spent time among both them and the Comanches—including their leader Quanah, who was himself part white.

Incredible stories about this relentless killer of men had spread among the Indians of the region just as they had among the whites. Some of the children who had a short time earlier been mocking and brutalizing him now ran for their homes; for he was the bogeyman their parents sometimes threatened them with to make them behave properly.

To keep children in line, they were told of a creature called *Pia Mupitsi: the Big Cannibal Owl*. They were warned that this monster that lived in a cave on the south side of the Wichita Mountains came out to eat bad children at night.

If the idea of being eaten alive failed to do the trick, parents would then threaten unruly offspring with the man called Kills Many.

"You might just as well have brought a *devil* into our homes!" Quanah accused Wolf Track.

"He's just another man," Wolf Track declared without true conviction, seeking desperately to save face. "He'll die as easily as any other."

"We'll talk about this tomorrow," Quanah replied, asserting his authority. "Until then," he swept his steely eyes over those gathered about, "no one is to touch him." He turned his back on them, so as to face the captive white man.

"That's all I can do for you, brother," he whispered to Jason, who nodded weakly in acknowledgment of the words.

Quanah turned away from him and walked back toward the village; all the others followed after him. The last to leave was Wolf Track, who fixed Mankiller with a baleful glare.

"Your death has only been delayed, white man," he vowed. "And now when it comes, it will be even slower and more painful." He seemed almost gleeful at the thought as he too then left to return to the encampment.

Left alone, Jason thought of the half-breed war chief who had granted him this brief reprieve. Nearly everyone in Texas knew at least part of the story of the man that they called Quanah Parker.

They knew of how a nine-year-old girl named Cynthia Ann Parker had been captured and taken away from home and family by the Comanches in May of 1836—just weeks after the fall of the Alamo, barely a month after the pivotal Battle of San Jacinto had won Texas independence from Mexico.

"He'll die as easily as any other."

Cynthia Ann was a blonde, with gentle blue eyes. Her captors gave her the name *Naudah*—*"Keeps Warm With Us"*—and when she was of age a warrior named Peta Nucona had made her one of his wives.

Soon thereafter, she gave him a son, Quanah, meaning *"Sweet Flower"*—for legend said he was born in a bed of wildflowers.

A second son, Pecos, followed him; and finally a daughter named Topsannah: "Prairie Flower."

Then, at the Battle of Peese River in 1860, a combined force of soldiers and Texas Rangers attacked a Comanche village. Among those the white men took captive were Cynthia Ann and her infant daughter.

The child did not fare well in white captivity and was dead before her tenth birthday. Cynthia Ann went to her own reward soon thereafter, still grieving for her two lost sons; Jason's strongest personal memory of her was of her being a loving mother. She never learned that her boys had escaped death or capture that day on the Peese.

Within a few short years of that battle, Peta Nucona and Pecos would also die, from grief and one of the white man's diseases, and Quanah would be left with no family.

His father had been well respected among the Comanches, highly regarded as a warrior. But he was also called by them "the Wanderer," and had no close friends.

Young Quanah too would be largely a loner, who chose as his domain the vast, barren wasteland known as the *Llano Estacado: the Staked Plains*.

He found another, more accepting home when a Comanche chief named Yellow Bear invited Quanah to join his camp. In time, Quanah took the chief's daughter Weekeah to be his first wife, then departed with some twenty other warriors to form his own band. He would become the chief of this band of Quahadi ("Antelope Eaters") Comanches.

Jason suspected Quanah's reputation as a leader had taken a severe hit just a few months earlier, when he directed the disastrous attack on the white trading post at Adobe Walls. That poorly executed assault had gone horribly, horribly wrong: with twenty-eight white men (mostly buffalo hunters) and one woman holding off two-hundred Indian warriors for three days, losing only one man for every day of the siege. Quanah would carry the scar from a wound he had sustained during the battle for the rest of his days. None could say if the wound to his heart ever healed.

Among the stubborn defenders of the trading depot was a young man who would go on to carve quite a reputation for himself in the West: Bat Masterson.

In a gruesome aftermath to the battle, when a relief column of soldiers arrived at Adobe Walls—they were greeted by the sight of the severed heads of thirteen Quahadi warriors displayed atop the wooden posts of the depot's corral.

If for no other reason than this, Mankiller was unsure if Quanah would be able to sway his tribesmen into sparing the white man's life. And it was clear that Wolf Track felt emboldened enough to challenge Quanah's standing as a leader of the village.

Yet even with tensions running high, the people of the camp chose to celebrate the relative success of Wolf Track's raid. Even amidst the sounds of revelry, though, Jason could hear cries of grief.

Grief over loved ones they knew might well have died by Mankiller's hands.

The celebration continued well into the night. Amazingly, even with all the noise it generated, even with all his pain and the prospect of far greater pain to come, Jason was able to will himself to sleep in fits and starts. Hard experience had taught him that, as with food, sleep was a precious commodity that must be grabbed whenever possible.

By the time the village grew completely dark and silent, Mankiller was fully alert. One of the last revelers to amble away to his lodge was Wolf Track; even at a distance Jason recognized his swagger and the guttural sound of a voice still raised in boastful bragging.

After allowing time for the villagers to all fall into deep sleep, Mankiller put into motion the desperate plan he had devised to attempt in order to affect an escape.

He started to swing slowly back and forth slightly, then threw his body upward as he had done involuntarily when the boy had kicked him in the groin.

As had happened then, when he fell back down the lodge pole to which he was tied bowed in the middle. Ignoring the resulting bolt of pain that shot through his upper body, he repeated this move again and again.

His breathing quickly became labored from the effort, and his naked body glistened with perspiration—but at last he was rewarded by hearing a slight cracking sound come from the sagging lodge pole.

He stopped moving, waiting to see if anyone in the village had also heard that telltale sound and would come to investigate. He also used that brief respite to rest and regain strength for renewed efforts.

When he saw no heads popping out of tipis, he again lurched upward, letting his full weight drag down on the pole as it bent in the downward arc. Again. Again.

And this time the pole snapped in two.

Jason dropped heavily to the ground; it was the first time his feet had touched blessed earth in hours. With the pole broken, the ropes that bound him to it loosened, and he was able to pull free.

The drifter had no feeling in his hands, but still he managed to grab hold of the shorter end of the broken lodge pole, meaning to use it and its jagged end as a makeshift spear if need be.

For several minutes he simply lay where he had fallen, allowing the circulation to return to his limbs. He twitched as the restored blood flow bit at his nerves like a swarm of angry ants.

Still no one in the village stirred.

When Jason did begin to move, it was not immediately away from the encampment. Alone and afoot in the wilderness, naked and armed only with a broken pole—his odds of survival would not be much greater than if he was still a trussed-up captive.

Remaining crouched low to the ground, he moved slowly and silently around the periphery of the village; taking great care to watch out for and avoid any camp dogs that might be prowling about.

His path took him behind one tipi that he could tell by the smells emanating from within must be the village's *Smoke Lodge*. This was a special tipi kept for men so old they no longer went on war parties. Here, they would gather each day to smoke and reminisce about the glory days of their youth. No boys or women were allowed within its confines.

Mankiller did not linger there, but continued on to the tipi that was his ultimate destination. He pressed his ear against its curved, buffalo hide "wall" and heard no sounds coming from inside.

With a look of grim determination on his face, Jason slithered into the lodge of Wolf Track.

CHAPTER 11

The following morning, Quanah Parker was awakened by the sound of unusually loud voices outside his lodge.

Scowling, he rolled from his side onto his back—and found himself looking straight up at the point of a knife hovering directly above his head.

He tensed, holding his breath in anticipation of seeing the blade flash down at his face. But as the sleep was quickly flushed from his eyes and his brain, he realized there was no one else there holding the knife in place.

Rather, it was hanging suspended from one of the lodge poles of his tipi by a thin rawhide string tied around its hilt. Hastily, Quanah rolled from under it and snatched it loose from the string. His features hardened as he examined the knife and realized it was one of his own.

Pushing aside the entry flap of his lodge, he rushed outside to see several of his tribesmen hurrying to join a group that had already gathered at the place where Jason Mankiller had been left tied the night before.

Quanah brusquely pushed his way through the cluster of stunned onlookers and saw at once what had them so disturbed.

Hanging from a branch of one of the trees, suspended by rawhide rope tied around his wrists—was the naked body of a dead man.

But it was not the body of Mankiller.

While all others hung back fearfully, Quanah approached the body, reaching under its chin and pushing its head up.

Both men and women cried out in horror, but Quanah was not surprised by what he saw.

The body was that of Wolf Track. His throat had been expertly sliced from ear to ear.

And his killer, doubtless using a finger dipped in the victim's own blood, had painted a crude *teardrop* running from the corner of Wolf Track's left eye and down his cheek.

"This is the work of Kills Many," one warrior muttered softly.

"Of course it is," Quanah replied.

"He couldn't have gone far," another said. "Should we go after him?" Quanah noted that even though the warrior had posed the question, he did not sound very enthusiastic about his own idea.

"No," Quanah said firmly. "Wolf Track was wrong to bring the white demon into our camp—and he's paid for that mistake. There's no need for anyone else to die."

He decided now was the time to speak to his people of another matter; one he had spent hours discussing with some of the sub-chiefs the previous night.

"We've received news that the Pony Soldiers of the white men are approaching our land in great numbers. They mean to make war on us.

"The remaining bands of Comanches and Kiowas have sent word that they mean to gather together to the north of here, to face the soldiers in battle." He paused to study the eyes and minds of his tribesmen.

"The Quahadi will join them," he declared firmly.

Quanah felt certain the timing of this announcement could not have been better. Among the Comanches, there was little mourning for the old who died naturally, but intense grieving for young men such as Wolf Track who perished. There was no time for mourning rituals now, though. For while the Comanches did not fear death, it did worry them—and they would often break camp after a burial to distance themselves from a place now associated with it.

Given the pronouncement Quanah had made, and eager to leave this place that now seemed cursed, the villagers quickly dispersed to begin the work of dismantling their lodges and preparing to move. Such was their incentive to do so that they would be on their way within an hour.

Two men cut down the slain Wolf Track and carried his body away to be prepared for quick disposal. As the other villagers hurried off to begin the work of dismantling the camp, Quanah remained for a time where he stood.

He closely examined the knife he still held in his hands: the one that had been left dangling over his head as he slept.

He knew it represented a message from the killer of men: one that was clear and unmistakable.

"Just as easily as I removed your rival Wolf Track, so too could I have killed you, brother. I spare you in the name of old friendship."

Quanah had now done the same for him.

Neither was in the other's debt.

CHAPTER 12

In a small Kiowa village, of the band called the *Kogui* (Elks), the warrior called Three Pony sat in front of his lodge, reclining slightly against a wooden back rest.

A young man of fewer than thirty summers, he wore his hair in the style favored by most Kiowa men: with a portion of it cut short over his right ear, but the rest long and braided, wrapped in strips of fur. At the moment, he was similarly wrapping his favorite bow with fresh sinew to strengthen it.

Three Pony paused in his labors as he heard crowd noises coming from the south end of the circle of tipis. Setting his work aside, he rose and casually sauntered over to see what was stirring the people.

What he saw when he got there was a lone rider, slowly entering the periphery of the tribe's circular encampment. Three Pony instantly recognized the rider, when his eyes lit upon the red tattoo rolling down the rider's left cheek.

Jason Mankiller's body clearly displayed every wound and contusion he had suffered in the past few days, for he wore no clothing save a breech cloth and moccasins he had taken from the lodge of Wolf Track. Around his waist he wore his own belt, holster, pistol and knife. He had been unable to find his Henry repeating rifle, but carried a single-shot, breech-loaded Spencer rifle he had likewise purloined from the late Wolf Track.

He was riding a sturdy black pony he had stolen from the Comanche village's herd and was leading a second horse: an amiable pinto. The pinto in turn was dragging behind it a crudely constructed travois.

The day before, Jason had come upon a lone buffalo cow and her calf of a little more than a year and had succeeded in downing them both. The butchered meat of the two animals was now resting on the travois, beneath their furry hides.

All that was missing was the cow's liver, which Mankiller had consumed raw in an effort to restore the blood and strength he had lost at the hands of the Comanches.

Still extremely weak and weary, he had made for this Kiowa encampment, the same one he had bypassed just days earlier, hoping that he would be made welcome here.

But seeing that the man astride the black pony was white, one of the villagers raised his rifle and took aim. Before he could pull the trigger, the weapon was batted down by Three Pony.

"Are you all blind?" Three Pony asked, pushing to the front of the gathering and facing them with his arms spread.

"Don't you recognize this man? He's the grandson of one of our own: she who was called Sparrow Wing Woman." He made a broad sweeping motion with one arm.

"He's known through all the world as Kills Many!" And many in the crowd reacted with awe at this revelation.

"And he's a brother," Three Pony concluded.

"A brother who comes bearing gifts," Jason cheerfully declared in the Kiowas' own tongue.

He nimbly hopped down off the black pony and greeted Three Pony by gripping his forearms.

"The spotted *sun dog*," he said, using the Kiowa term for horse, "is for Three Pony, my friend and brother.

"The buffalo meat it carries—is for any who want it!"

He knew full well that cherished buffalo were becoming more and more scarce on the Plains—by deliberate design.

The Treaty of Medicine Lodge, signed in 1867, had included a provision making it unlawful for any whites to hunt buffalo in the lands south of the Arkansas River. Once the great herds to the north became depleted, though—and with the prospect of earning four dollars for every shaggy hide they brought in—white hunters in large numbers chose to ignore the prohibition.

Nor did the U.S. military make any real effort to deter this illegal practice. General Phil Sheridan had personally expressed the opinion that the quickest, easiest and surest way to deal with "the vexed Indian question" was simply to destroy "the Indian commissary:" the buffalo.

Still, for all their love of the succulent meat of the bison, pride now prevented the Kiowas from taking advantage of Jason's largesse—momentarily.

"Let me through!" shouted a gruff but female voice.

Showing the sense common to women but rare in men, one of the females of the village elbowed her way to the travois and threw back the hides covering its contents.

"Give the hides to your chiefs," Jason said to her.

"They're welcome to them!" she declared loudly, ignoring the hides and scooping up a large slab of hump meat.

As if a dam had burst, other women now surged forward, eager to claim the other cuts of meat.

"Fix a fine meal," Three Pony shouted to them, "and put on your finest dresses. Tonight, we'll celebrate the return of our brother, Kills Many!"

He then let out an ululating yelp. Other warriors took up the cry: a few fired shots in the air.

As the women continued to scramble for meat, Three Pony threw a solicitous arm around Jason's shoulders and led him away.

"You don't look so good, brother," he said to the drifter.

"I don't feel so good, either," Jason admitted. "I've been a guest of the Quahadis—who didn't make me feel nearly so welcome as you have."

"Great fighters they are," Three Pony commented, "but sometimes lacking in the social graces."

"You got that right, pardner," Jason said. "So I could sure use a soft place to lay down for awhile."

"You need more than that," Three Pony said firmly, eyeing Jason's many injuries and wounds; a few of them still oozed pus and blood. The concern the Kiowa felt was evident in his eyes.

"You'll rest in my lodge," he told Jason, "and my wives will nurse you. Stay as long as you like with us; you'll be safe here." He pulled the white man closer to him and smiled.

"You're home now."

CHAPTER 13

That night, the tribe held as big a party as they could muster. They'd had little cause for celebration of late; most of their fellow Kiowas had recently finally given up and given in. They now languished on a reservation to the north, in the Indian Territory.

As was common at such festivities, several of the men regaled their audience with thrilling stories of their past great deeds, always to great acclamation.

"I'd like to hear a story from you, Kills Many," one of them said at last, leaning toward Jason. "One story in particular."

"What story is that?" Mankiller inquired, slightly puzzled.

"Several times now," the man said pointedly, "Three Pony has told us the tale of how you two first met. He told us the two of you were set upon by no less than ten white men, out for blood. He told us the two of you killed them all—five apiece." The man's eyes shifted toward Three Pony.

"Now, I'm sure we'd all like to hear *your* version of the story."

Three Pony looked a little stricken upon hearing this request, for he of course knew that the actual facts of that first encounter were vastly different from the story he had been telling his tribesmen.

The truth was that a mere two cowboys had caught Three Pony after he had killed a stray maverick steer, captured the Kiowa and prepared to lynch him. Jason had come along just in time to prevent the hanging and had sent the two cowhands scurrying away without ever firing a shot.

Mankiller now leaned forward toward the central campfire and a dozen or so pairs of eyes followed him; clearly, they were anxious to hear if his account jibed with that given by Three Pony. Jason took his time, knowing he had a rapt and captive audience. He said nothing for a long moment, letting the suspense build.

"First of all," he began at last, " let me start by saying that my memory of that particular incident differs from that of my brother's." At these words, several of the men grinned and Three Pony began to visibly squirm.

"Three Pony is being far too modest in his telling of the story," Jason said with a straight face.

"The truth is…I only killed *four* men that day. Three Pony killed *six* of the white devils."

He then proceeded to go into great, lurid, gruesome—and totally fictional—detail about this supposed epic fight.

"The final two," Jason concluded, reaching out with both hands and grabbing at the air, "Three Pony killed with his bare hands!"

As enthralled by this fantastical narrative as were the other members of his tribe, Three Pony jerked erect when he realized their eyes were now all trained on him. Smiling and puffing out his chest, he emphatically nodded his agreement with Jason's version of their meeting.

One of the other warriors let out a yelp of approval, and many others followed his example. Again shots were fired into the air.

Three Pony looked gratefully at Mankiller, who gave him a sly wink in reply.

Some time later, as the celebratory feast and mood were winding down, a tribesman named Red Hand posed another question to their guest of honor.

"Two days from now," he told the drifter, "most of us men will be leaving the village. We're going to join forces with Quanah Parker's band of Quahadi, and make war against the Pony Soldiers.

"But some of us," Red Hand's gaze shifted toward one of the older sub-chiefs who was seated near Jason on his right side: a man called Flies North. "Some of us have counseled against doing this."

"He means me," Flies North said stiffly. He leaned toward Jason, displaying a large trinket he wore on a chain. Mankiller recognized it as being a so-called "Peace Medal."

"The White Father himself put this around my neck," Flies North declared, "after he brought me and other chiefs to visit him in his big white house."

"And ever since Flies North returned from that journey," Red Hand asserted, "he has told us we have no hope of stopping the white men."

"Does he speak truly," another man asked, "or has he just grown too old and tired to fight?" Flies North bristled at these words, but said nothing.

Jason hesitated before answering, wanting to choose his words carefully. He well knew the main purpose of such "peace" missions as the old sub-chief had described.

Place an Indian who has never seen anything faster than a horse on a roaring, rushing train. Show him just how vast is the territory already owned by the whites; how many and how large are their cities; how large is their population. Impress upon them the hopelessness of resistance.

"Flies North has spoken truly to you," the bounty hunter sadly confirmed.

"Not only do the whites have weapons that can shake the whole earth, but they also have more people, more soldiers than there are stars in the sky.

"Many of you know about the Battle Between Brothers that the whites of the north and south fought not ten summers past. There were many times during that war that they would kill each other by the thousands in a single day...and then do the same thing the very next day.

"They did this for *four years*—yet all the dead represented no greater loss to them than the heavens would feel if one star was snuffed out.

"The village of Washington, where the White Father lives, is so big and so crowded that if a great hand swept all its people away and replaced them with the whole Kiowa nation—it would not be enough to fill half of that village back up.

"And that's just one of their villages. They have many, many more; some even bigger, with even more people living in them."

His words caused a murmuring among his listeners. Red Hand, not wanting to believe what had been said to them, glared at the drifter.

"No offense, brother," he said, "but you're mostly a white man yourself. How do we know you've spoken the truth?"

"Ask Flies North," Mankiller replied, turning his eyes toward the sub-chief. "Do I lie, father?"

Flies North shook his head.

This was deeply sobering to the Kiowas, and the gathering grew silent.

"Even if it's so," Red Hand spoke up at last, "even if it's hopeless...I'd rather die in one last, great battle than live a long life on a reservation!"

Several of the younger men yelped their agreement. The older men and women maintained their silence.

"What about you, Kills Many?" Red Hand said, extending a hand toward Jason. "Will you join us in the battle? It would be an honor for you and us both. Together, we'll make the Pony Soldiers cry blood!"

All the other warriors whooped gleefully, seconding the motion.

Even if it hadn't been in a hopeless cause, Mankiller had no intention of waging war on the side of the Indians; but he knew it was crucial that he choose the right words in rejecting their overture.

"You honor me just by asking," he said finally. "Any man would be proud to ride into battle with the Kiowas; none are braver in war than they are. But I'm in the middle of my own war." He made a sweeping gesture with one arm.

"My path carries me elsewhere—after three men I have to kill."

Red Hand nodded at these words. No one there doubted Mankiller's bravery; and it was the Indian way to accept the decision of any man who chose not to join a war party, without recrimination.

A warrior could decline to join a fight for any reason, or for no reason, without shame.

The Indians' lack of any sort of military structure, discipline or strategy was one of the things that put them at such a disadvantage against the white men's war machine. Still, Jason deeply admired their sense of individual initiative and pursuit of life.

"Hey!" Three Pony called out loudly, attempting to dispel the suddenly somber mood. "Battles are for tomorrow—tonight is for celebrating!"

As if in reply, several of the women came rushing forward to replenish plates of food. One young woman smiled warmly at Jason as she offered him a dish much favored by the Kiowas: a sort of sweet mush consisting of buffalo bone marrow mixed with crushed mesquite beans. He accepted it gratefully.

As the festivities resumed, Mankiller leaned close to Three Pony. "Follow my example, brother. Stay home and don't go to war."

Three Pony shrugged fatalistically. "What else can I do—resign myself to digging in the dirt and eating cows?"

"I suppose not," Mankiller said, reaching over and squeezing his friend's arm.

"No more than I can."

CHAPTER 14

Lee Burris had quickly fallen in love with this vast, unspoiled land; so much so that when the survey team he led finished its business he sent the rest of the men back to their base camp while he chose to remain behind for an extra day or two and just enjoy the solitude.

He paused in stirring the pot of beans he was cooking over his small campfire, inhaling its aroma. Out here in the open, even the simplest of fare seemed to taste better to him.

Burris was startled but unconcerned when he looked up to see two strange men come walking into the circle of his fire's light. They were both scruffy, tough-looking men: unwashed and unshaved. Not so unusual in appearance, he reasoned, out on the frontier.

Both men were afoot, though one of them was leading a buckskin horse by its reins.

"Good evening, gents," Burris said in a welcoming voice.

"Evenin'," the one leading the horse replied. He was the taller of the two, with a nose that looked like it had been broken on multiple occasions.

"What can I do for you?" the surveyor asked.

"Muh horse went lame a way's back," the shorter of the strangers said. "We had ta put 'im down."

"That's too bad," Burris replied. He pointed to the bubbling pot on the campfire. "All I've got at the moment to share with you is some beans; but you're welcome to it."

"That's right neighborly of ya," the taller stranger said. "But you got a lot more than just beans." In a smooth motion he pulled his pistol and pointed it at the stunned surveyor. His partner did likewise.

"And we mean ta take it all."

Burris' reeling brain barely had time to register the fact that he was going to die when two shots rang out in the night.

Neither of them had been fired by the pair of would-be outlaws.

Rather, the gunshots had come from somewhere behind Burris, and both had struck home.

The shorter of the two strangers quickly crumpled in a heap to the ground. The taller one swayed but stayed on his feet—until a third shot threw him backwards and finished the job.

Near paralyzed with fear, Burris risked looking back over his left shoulder in time to see a new figure step out of the concealing darkness. The surveyor's heart sank: it seemed he had not been saved so much as merely been delivered into the hands of savage Indians.

Yet it was no Indian who had fired the fatal shots, but rather Jason Mankiller. He still wore a breechcloth and moccasins, but now also sported a long, buckskin shirt presented to him as a parting gift by Three Pony. He stopped next to Burris, but his eyes remained locked on the fallen outlaws.

"I mean you no harm, pilgrim," he said softly.

In long strides he crossed the small clearing, walking over to the prone thieves and giving each one a sharp kick in the ribs. When the shorter of the two moaned and twitched slightly, Jason put a second bullet into him, causing Burris to jump nervously.

Mankiller knelt beside the dead outlaws, studying their ugly faces.

He recognized neither of them from any wanted posters, nor were either of them one of the Comancheros he hunted: so they were of no further interest to him.

He lifted each in turn and slung their limp bodies over the back of the buckskin horse before leading the animal off into the dark.

Burris sat anxiously waiting for the next half-hour, wondering what was transpiring beyond the range of his sight or hearing. He jumped anew when a voice called out to him from the night's cover.

"Hello, the camp. I'm coming back in."

When Mankiller stepped into the light of the surveyor's camp, he was still leading the buckskin; but of the two dead outlaws it had been carrying there was now no sign.

Burris noticed that his rescuer was also now wearing trousers—doubtless taken from one of his victims. For the first time, Lee got a good look at the face of the drifter; saw that it showed signs of recent and harsh abuse. He stared openly at the teardrop tattoo on the man's cheek.

"My name's Jason Mankiller," the tattooed man said, finally making a formal greeting.

"I'm Lee Burris." The surveyor felt he should know the name "Mankiller," but such recollection eluded him. His eyes flicked to one side. "Did you bury them?"

Mankiller snorted derisively.

"Hell, no. I just took 'em far enough away that you and me shouldn't be bothered by the scavengers they'll attract, and I dumped 'em there." He glanced down at the still simmering pot of beans and licked his lips.

"Mind if I share your camp, Mr. Burris?"

"Of course, of course," Burris said hastily. Dumbfounded and still a little mistrustful and even afraid of this third stranger of the evening, he nonetheless felt obligated to extend him that courtesy.

"I suppose they did deserve what they got," he said, averting his eyes as he stirred the pot.

"They surely did."

"Still," Burris said hesitantly. "The way you did it...I mean, I know they were outlaws, cutthroats. But you just gunned them down in cold blood, without any warning."

"That I did," Jason said nonchalantly. "Just the same as they intended to do to you. Would you rather I'd let them?"

"No...no! Of course not," Burris stammered. "I'm sorry, Mr. Mankiller. I didn't mean to sound ungrateful. You saved my life, and I thank you."

"I can tell you this, pilgrim; I won't lose a wink o' sleep over the two of 'em," Jason said to him. "And neither should you." He cocked his head slightly to one side, as if studying the surveyor.

"You're new out here, aren't you?"

"Fairly."

"Well, let this be a lesson, then. Here in the West, it's considered good etiquette to call out a warning to a man before you enter his camp or his house, like I just did for you.

"The fact that those two owlhoots failed to extend you that courtesy should have told you that they didn't have good intentions."

"I see."

"And you should always keep your gun close to hand, even when you're bedding down for the night."

Burris looked slightly embarrassed. "But I don't have a gun."

Shaking his head incredulously, Mankiller dug into the buckskin's saddlebags and removed a gunbelt and pistol he had liberated from one of the slain outlaws.

"Now you do," he said, tossing it to Burris, who caught it clumsily. "Make sure you wear it or at least keep it within easy reach when you're in the wild."

Burris stood, strapping on the gunbelt and pushing it down on his hips.

"You got any money on you, pilgrim?" Jason asked.

Burris froze: his heart sinking as the suspicion rose in him that he might still be the victim of a hold-up. Even though he was now armed, he was certain he'd stand no chance of outdrawing this strange visitor to his camp.

"Only a couple of dollars," he managed to croak.

Mankiller laughed dryly. "Then, except for your horse that those two wanted, you got even less than they did!" He then fished twenty dollars in folding money out of his pants pocket, counted out half of it and handed it over to the amazed surveyor.

"You took that off those men?" Burris said, staring down at the money in his hand as if inspecting it for bloodstains.

"Yep."

"But…but isn't that *stealing*?"

Jason laughed more deeply. "Stealing from *who*, exactly? You can be purty sure it wasn't earned honest by those two scofflaws to begin with; nor is there any way to finds its original and rightful owner.

"And those two sure ain't got no further use for it."

"Still," Burris demurred, trying to hand the money back to Mankiller, "you did all the work, so to speak. You should keep all the money."

"Fergit it," Jason said, shaking his head. "A man alone like you are needs a few dollars in his poke. You just take it; for the trouble they put you to."

Burris found himself smiling slightly, figuring he probably had far more money back home than did this poor drifter. Then he shrugged and stuffed the money into the pocket of his shirt.

"Sit, sit, Mr. Mankiller," he said.

"Mr. Mankiller was my daddy. Call me Jason."

"And I'm Lee. The beans are nearly done; but if you don't mind waiting a little while longer, I can whip us up a decent batch of biscuits to go along with them."

"I allow as that would suit me just fine, Lee."

He left the camp for just a minute to retrieve the Indian pony he had left tied up. From a pouch he had slung over its back he pulled out a few strips of dried venison. When he had departed from the Kiowa village the day before, Three Pony's wives had given this to him, along with a pouch of pemmican and a water skin. They had tried to press even more upon him; but knowing how poor their village was, he had refused them.

He tossed a few strips of the venison into the pot, letting it stew and soften in the bean broth while the two men waited for the biscuits to bake. As they began to partake of their simple but filling meal, Jason could see the man he'd rescued begin to relax in his presence.

"Tell me, Jason," the surveyor said, wiping at his mouth with the back of his right hand, "whereabouts is it that you call home?"

Mankiller shrugged. "Ever since the war ended, 'home' to me has mostly just been the place I happen to be spreading my bedroll. I guess the closest to a stay-in-one-place home I have at the moment, though, is a little town to the east of here, called Fort Rogers." Burris' eyebrows arched slightly at the mention of it.

"Nice place, is it?" he asked.

"Nice enough for me," Jason replied. "I only stayed there a short while, back in the spring, but I kinda took a likin' to it. That's where I'm headed now."

Burris smiled on hearing this, an idea springing into his mind. "Mr. Mankiller," he said lightly, "I think we need to talk about me repaying you for all the help you've been to me."

"We don't need to do no such of a thing, Lee," Jason replied adamantly. "You've freely shared your grub, your company and your camp with me. That's enough."

"...whereabouts is it you call home?"

"That's poor reward for saving a man's life," Burris persisted. "I think I can maybe do more; and I intend to."

"Suit yerself, pilgrim," Jason said, holding out his empty tin plate. "You gonna eat the rest o' them beans?"

CHAPTER 15

A day and nearly a half later found Mankiller again alone on the trail. He was now riding the buckskin stallion he had "inherited" from the slain outlaw, and was leading the black Indian pony on a rope.

He reined in his mount, tensing as he heard what sounded like the yapping of an agitated dog coming from ahead and around a bend in the trail. He pulled his Spencer rifle from its scabbard before slowly proceeding onward.

The noise led him to a rather grim discovery, as he came upon the remains of a solitary Studebaker wagon. It was partially destroyed; one wheel had fallen off and many of the wagon's contents lay scattered about on the ground. The horses that had pulled it were long gone.

As the drifter dismounted and cautiously approached the scene, he saw the source of the yapping noise: a tiny mongrel dog, no bigger than an alley cat. One end of a rope was tied around its scrawny neck; the other end of the rope was secured to the rear axle of the wagon.

There was clear sign that the wagon and whatever travelers it had transported had been the victims of an Indian raid: arrows could still be seen protruding from the Studebaker's sides and canvas top.

Jason wondered idly why the raiders hadn't bothered to kill the dog. Maybe they thought it was crazy, he mused, given its wild caterwauling and the drunken way it skipped and hopped back and forth. Most Indians sought to avoid close contact with crazy critters—two-legged or otherwise.

"It's all right, little fella," the man said soothingly, slowly approaching the dog, which continued its frantic efforts to pull free of the restraining rope.

Jason tentatively reached a hand out toward the trapped animal, only to yank it back quickly as the understandably mistrustful dog snarled and snapped at him.

Casting his eyes about, Mankiller saw pots, pans and the like lying on the ground nearby: objects the Indians had not felt inclined to take with them. Snatching up a shallow tin pie pan, he filled it with some of the contents of the water skin that hung from the horn of his saddle.

"Let's see if we can't get you in a better mood," he said softly to the dog. He placed the tin on the ground and used one foot to slowly push it toward the dog, who retreated a short distance but continued its barking.

Only when Jason turned and walked several feet away did the parched but suspicious pup ease toward the tin. Keeping one eye on the man, it sniffed at the water in the pie pan and then began to eagerly lap it up.

With the poor pooch thus otherwise occupied for the moment, Jason took a closer look around the rest of the immediate area. It was but a moment before he discovered the body of a white man.

The corpse had been stripped and then mutilated: part of the scalp along with various body parts were missing. In addition to whatever wound had killed the man, several arrows had been shot into him post-mortem.

As he dreaded, Mankiller found the remains of a second victim in the underbrush nearby. It was a woman; probably the dead man's wife. What her attackers had done to her was even more unspeakable.

Returning to the wagon, he found the little mongrel to have calmed down a bit. It still growled lowly at him, but he noticed it had emptied the pie tin. Striding over to his buckskin, the drifter retrieved the entire water skin and also withdrew a few strips of venison from his saddlebag.

He squatted down near the dog, so it could see him chewing at a piece of the dried meat, smell it. He then tossed a piece of the venison to the pooch, which initially recoiled from it but then devoured it as ferociously as he had the water.

"Now, let's try this again," Mankiller said, slowly approaching the mongrel and holding out another strip of meat toward it. The dog snatched it from his fingers but made no attempt to bite the man.

Jason poured some more water into the pie pan. As the dog lowered its head to lap up the liquid, Mankiller deftly flicked out his skinning knife and cut the rope from the mongrel's neck.

Feeling its restraint vanish, the dog took off running, as Jason expected it would. As it disappeared into the underbrush, the drifter climbed into the back of the wagon and began to sift through the few contents that hadn't been stolen or tossed outside.

He came upon a shovel, which he set to one side. He also discovered a small leather pouch containing a handful of coins. Absent finding a family Bible or any other documents that might have identified the dead couple or their next of kind, he shoved the pouch into his own pocket.

Exiting the wagon, shovel in hand, he was mildly surprised to find the little dog had returned. It sat quietly on its haunches now, staring up expectantly at him. The drifter knelt beside the pooch; allowed it to sniff and lick at his hand, then gave it a good scratching behind its ears.

The pooch followed along behind Mankiller and watched as he began to dig a grave. Jason found the work tough going in the dry, hard soil: his privations at the hands of the Comanches had left him still weaker than normal.

Because of this, he considered digging just one common grave for the two slain travelers: it wasn't as if anyone but him would ever know or care. But thinking of his own parents and what he would have wanted for them even if they had not died in separate times and places, he quickly dismissed the idea and kept digging.

Though panting heavily from the effort, he did not allow himself to stop until he had two holes sufficiently deep to keep the bodies safe from any scavengers that might otherwise dig them up.

He cut swatches of canvas from the wagon's cover: wrapping the bodies in them before gently lowering them into their graves. He even took the time to fashion two crude crosses from boards ripped from the side of the Studebaker and lashed together with pieces of the rope that had bound the dog.

After filling them in, Jason stood silently over the two graves for a moment, head bowed. Part of him felt he should say a few words over them as well. But though his dear mother had taken pains to acquaint him with the Bible as a boy, he was unschooled in any sort of organized religion; and thus felt unqualified and unworthy of doing so.

Finally, he refilled the dog's improvised water dish and set a few slices of his precious venison next to it. After giving the pooch one last scratch, he mounted his horse and resumed his journey.

Mankiller had not gone far before he realized that the little dog was following him as best it could. He tried to ignore it, figuring it would soon tire and go its own way to fend for itself like every other animal in the wild. The pooch was game, he had to admit; but its short, stubby legs were no match for those of Jason's horses even though they were only moving at a leisurely walking pace. The dog quickly fell behind them.

The drifter reined in his buckskin as he reached the crest of a low rise and took a look back over his shoulder. The little mongrel was still on his tail, tiny legs pumping away.

When it caught up to Jason it sat back on its haunches, looking up at him plaintively. The dog was panting heavily, tongue hanging out of its mouth. Jason averted his eyes, gazing out over the empty horizon. Then he looked back down at the pooch.

"Aw, hell," the man growled.

He leaned over to one side as far as he could without falling out of the saddle, grabbed the mongrel by the scruff of its neck and lifted it up off the ground, placing it in front of him on his perch atop the buckskin.

The dog squirmed a little, adjusting itself and finding a comfortable position before settling down and resting its head on its front paws.

It seemed content.

CHAPTER 16

On the front porch of the simple hut that was her home, the little girl named Anita Maria Mendoza played happily with her most prized possession: a stuffed doll that had been given to her by the man she knew as "Senor Jason." At the moment, Anita was playing the role of a mother: scolding her "child" for some imaginary transgression.

The girl paused in her play to wipe away beads of sweat from her tiny forehead. It had been a long, hot summer in this part of Texas; and the fall had not brought much relief.

All the vegetation around the hut was in shades of brown and yellow, and crunched underfoot when you stepped upon it. The ground was baked hard.

As Anita glanced up from her play, she was surprised to see a man on horseback slowly approaching. Her surprise turned to delight as he drew close enough to be recognized.

"Mama! Mama!" the little girl shrieked. "Senor Jason has come back!"

Mankiller reined in his buckskin as the child raced up to greet him. She was barely tall enough to reach his boot, but she reached out and hugged his leg firmly.

"Hello, poppet," he said to her, smiling warmly.

Anita began to hop up and down, holding her arms up to him. He obliged by leaning down and lifting her up onto his saddle with one strong arm. Once there, she embraced his neck so tightly his breath caught; then kissed him several times on the cheek.

"I love the dolly you gave me," she told him excitedly, holding up the simple toy for him to see. "I play with her every day!"

Before the drifter could make reply, he heard the sound of the hut's front door opening. He swiveled his head to see Anita's mother, Rosario, step out onto the porch. Dressed in a billowing red skirt and white blouse, her dark hair framing a pretty face, she appeared to him almost like a rose in an otherwise barren desert.

She smiled at him, and he nodded in greeting.

"I was passing close by," he said as the woman stepped down from the porch and walked toward him, "and thought I'd just stop by and see how you two ladies were doin'.

"I hope you're not put out, what with me just showing up unannounced and uninvited."

"You're always welcome here, Jason," Rosario said sincerely. "You'll join us for supper."

"I'd be pleasured to."

By now, little Anita had discovered the mongrel dog nesting on Jason's saddle. It gave no resistance as she picked it up in her arms and held it alongside her doll.

"Oooh," the child cooed. "Where did you find him?"

"I guess you could say we kinda found each other."

"Are you gonna keep him?" the girl asked guilelessly. "'Cause if you're not..." she turned her big brown eyes up to him. "Well...I had a birthday while you were gone."

"Anita Maria!" her mother gasped in horror. Anita ignored her, keeping her gaze locked on Jason's.

"To tell you the God's honest truth, chickabiddy," Mankiller said, likewise ignoring the mother for the moment, "I'm not much of a pet person. So I thought I'd give the little fella to *you*...if that's all right with your mama, of course."

Excited beyond imagining by the very prospect, Anita hugged the pooch so hard it whimpered.

"Can I keep him, Mama?" she pleaded, her voice quivering. "Please?"

Rosario shot a rather exasperated glare at Jason, who simply shrugged in mock innocence.

"I suppose you can," she surrendered, eliciting a squeal of delight from the girl. "But you listen to me, Anita. You'll have to take care of him: give him food and water."

"I will, Mama. Every day."

"And you hear me good, child. If that thing kills any of my chickens—I'll pluck and cook *it*!"

Rosario's features then softened as she placed a hand on Jason's leg and looked up at him. "Stable your horses in the shed and get washed up; supper will be ready soon."

Later, after the finest meal he'd had in months, Mankiller sat on the front porch of the hut with mother and child, enjoying the relative cool of the evening.

"I wanna thank you for that larrupin' supper, Rosario," he told the woman. "You're as good a cook as I remembered. Not enough chiles and peppers to set a man on fire, but enough to warm him good from gullet to gut."

"I'm glad you liked it," she said, accepting the rough compliment as it was intended.

Next to Jason, Anita was joyfully playing with her new pup, teasing him as you would a cat, with a colorful ribbon she dangled just out of reach of his paws and jaws. Suddenly, the girl's own jaw tightened as a most important question popped into her tiny head.

"Senor Jason," she asked. "What is his name?"

"Being that the two of us was never properly introduced," he told her, "I don't rightly know that he's even got one.

"I reckon that means you can call him whatever you want, child."

Anita cupped the squirming pooch's head in her hands and studied his face intently as Jason and Rosario exchanged covert smiles.

"I'm going to call him Hector," the girl declared emphatically.

"Hector?" Jason repeated, frowning slightly at the prospect. "Why Hector?"

"Because he looks like a Hector."

"Ya don't say." Mankiller picked up the dog and looked into its bright eyes, appearing to study the situation as seriously as had the child.

"By golly, you're right, sweet pea," he told her at last. "He *does* look like a Hector!"

"And now it's time for Hector to go to bed," Rosario said, rising to her feet. "And for little girls too, Anita."

"Aw, Mama," the child protested.

"You heard me." Rosario clapped her hands. "Scoot!"

The woman stood in the open doorway of the hut, keeping watch to make sure her instructions were being followed. She remained there for several minutes: as she had expected, both child and pup drifted off to sleep very quickly.

"I'll fix you a pallet on the floor," she told Jason, moving to stand beside where he still sat.

"No need to trouble yourself," he told her. "It'll do me just fine to sleep in the shed with the horses."

"The shed was fine when you were a stranger," she said firmly. "But now you're a friend—and you'll sleep in the house."

"All right," he replied, sensing it would do no good to argue the point with her further.

Reaching down, he plucked a few long blades of yellowed grass. So dry and brittle were they that they practically turned to powder when he closed his fist around them.

"The land around here seems mighty poor," he observed.

"Not as poor as you look," Rosario said, reaching out and lightly touching the discolored skin below his right eye. His many injuries had only just begun to heal and were still quite evident.

"You look horrible," the woman declared bluntly. "What happened to you?"

"Nothin' that time won't heal," he replied, brushing aside her concerns. "But about your land –?"

"It's not good," Rosario admitted. "We're in the third year of a drought." She hesitated, as if embarrassed to go on.

"If not for the money you left behind the last time you visited…I'm not sure what Anita and I would have done."

They sat together in silence for a time, until Mankiller decided to speak what was on his mind.

"I know that this is the place where your husband meant for you to live—but does it have a deep hold on you?"

"Not really. We hadn't lived here long when the dysentery took Tomas. It has not been a place of joy."

Jason grimaced with guilt. He felt it likely that the woman was now not only thinking of her dead husband but also of the brutal attack visited upon her by two outlaws after they left Mankiller for dead in the nearby wilderness. An attack witnessed by her innocent daughter and for which the drifter still felt partially responsible.

The fact that he had tracked the two human animals down and killed them had done little to salve his conscience where the mother and child were concerned.

"Why do you ask?" Rosario said, intruding upon his self-recrimination.

He struggled a bit internally before responding to her; afraid he would speak wrong.

"Why don't you and little Anita leave here?"

"Leave? But we have no other family; where would we go?"

"Come with me."

He held up a hand when she looked at him somewhat quizzically. "I'm not suggesting anything improper, Rosario," he assured her. "But I'm headed for Fort Rogers. It's a nice place. Strugglin' a bit, like lots of other places since the Depression, but it's getting better. And pretty soon it'll be getting bigger, too.

"I've recommended it to other folks as well. It's even got a nice Mexican community in it that I think would welcome you and the little one: make you feel ta home. I'm sure we can find you a place there that'll be better than this."

Safer, too, he thought but did not voice.

"You're a good man, Jason," Rosario said, smiling softly. "Kind, in your own way. I'll think on it."

"That's fair enough."

The woman held out a hand to him.

"Now, let's get to bed."

CHAPTER 17

In the Fort Rogers saloon called The Last Stand, it was still too early in the afternoon for business to be very brisk. The owner of the saloon, Sam Dobbins, stood behind the bar, using a towel to wipe down a surface that was already clean and dry.

His establishment sat on a prime location in what the locals called *Tiger Town*. The name derived from the many saloons there—in all of which any man feeling lucky could "buck the tiger:" play the game of chance called faro.

Standing across the bar from him was the gambler Cash Carpenter, who was already decked out in his "work clothes:" black broadcloth suit, boots and tie. Under the coat he wore a white shirt and a flashy silk vest. The cut of his coat concealed the shoulder holster wherein he carried his short barreled .38 caliber pistol.

Large diamond rings adorned the ring finger of his left hand and the pinky of his right. In the center of his tie rested a "headlight:" a stickpin with a large ruby set in it.

Beside Cash stood his older cousin Newt. He was the reason in large part why Cash had made this town his home base. Not only was Newt

Carpenter family; he was also a deputy to the town's marshal, making the law favorable to Cash.

"I have to say, Cousin," Cash told him, his Southern drawl flowing out of his mouth like mellifluous honey, "I expected you'd be holding the office of marshal yourself by now."

"That mighta been the case," Newt said, his voice coarser and more gravelly than his relative's, " if not for your friend Jason Mankiller."

"Whatever do you mean?" Cash asked.

"Once word got around that Marshal Russell had stood toe-to-toe with Mankiller and was even willing to take him on, people started looking at him in a whole new light.

"It was because of that as much as anything that the City Council voted unanimously to return him as marshal when his term expired a few weeks back."

"Too bad for you, Newt."

"Oh, that don't bother me none. I like the marshal; I still think I can stand to learn a thing or two from him.

"Besides, the fact that I was right there with him when he had his showdown with the bounty man drove up my own stock with the councilmen."

"The way I heard it," Cash interjected, "you weren't just there, Newt. You actually stepped between them and stopped more bloodshed."

The deputy remembered well the night he and the marshal had been urgently summoned to Bucktooth Bertha Hansen's whorehouse. They'd entered the foyer of the establishment just in time to see Jason Mankiller descending the steps from the upstairs rooms. He'd been dragging behind him the naked, lifeless corpse of a wanted outlaw named Tyrone McClure.

Newt now shrugged, or shuddered. "If I hadn't done so," he told his cousin, "I have no doubt Mankiller woulda done in the marshal and maybe me, too.

"And I'll tell you, Cash: that set-to surely left Marshal Russell a changed man."

"How so?"

"Before that, old Clay had kinda let hisself go, if you know what I mean. Just marking time till he could retire. Now, though, he seems to have more of the fire in his belly.

"It's made working for him more of a pleasure."

Newt was nursing a single mug of beer, since he was scheduled to go on duty in a couple of hours. Cash felt no such restraint, and now knocked back the remnants of a champagne flip.

Newt took silent note of the fact that his always-flamboyant cousin seemed to indulge in spirits a bit more than he used to since returning to town following his narrow escape from the Comanches. Not that Newt blamed him.

"Would you like a refill, Mr. Carpenter?" asked the bartender; a short man named Trey Revell. He unconsciously twirled one end of his waxed moustache as he spoke.

"Actually," Cash replied, "I think I'd like to try something a little different. Might you know how to concoct a Tom and Jerry?"

"Of course, sir," Revell said. "One Tom and Jerry coming right up."

As the bartender went about his business, Cash spoke to the saloon owner. "My compliments, Sam, on your new and more varied varieties of beverages."

"It's all part of my plan to increase business, Cash," Dobbins beamed. "And it seems to be paying off well.

"And one of the wisest moves I ever made was hiring Revell there and bringing him down from Kansas City. He's even training some of my other bartenders in what he calls the art of 'mixology'."

Revell returned with Cash's fresh drink and watched as the gambler took a sip.

"Is your drink satisfactory, sir?"

"Delightful," Cash responded, dragging out the first syllable. He lifted his glass to Sam Dobbins in a toast. "To art."

A movement caught Cash's eye and he turned to one side to see Jane Starr descending the stairs from their shared room on the second floor. She was dressed in an elegant black dress, which sharply set off the string of pearls she wore around her slender neck.

Cash raised his glass to her as well; she nodded in acknowledgment and walked over to join him and the others at the bar.

"Gentlemen," she said by way of greeting.

Before any could reply, a townsman came bursting excitedly in through the saloon's batwing doors.

"Hey, ever'body! You ain't gonna believe yer eyes!" he yelled loudly. "Jason Mankiller's comin' inta town!"

The first bar patron to reach the doors was Jane, a broad, bright smile on her lips.

But what she saw when she got there gave her pause; the smile froze in place and then faded.

It was an odd little caravan they all saw coming slowly down Front Street. At its head was Mankiller, still riding the buckskin he took off the outlaw he had killed. He was also still dressed in his conflicting wardrobe of jeans, moccasins and Indian shirt.

Sitting on the saddle in front of him was a small Mexican girl, who in turn was holding a little mongrel dog.

Beside them, on a burro, rode Rosario Mendoza. A rope tied to Jason's saddle horn led back to the black Indian pony coming up behind them. Carried on its back were Rosario and Anita's meager belongings.

"Thank God," Cash muttered earnestly. "I was afraid he'd made the big jump."

"I'm not sure there's anything or anyone that *can* kill him," Jane murmured softly; but loudly enough that others heard and would begin to spread the word that this man who cried blood could not be killed by any human means.

"If that don't take the rag off the bush," Newt Carpenter said cheerfully. "Not only is he alive—but he's done got him a *woman!*"

Jane turned on her heels and walked toward the table where her faro set-up awaited. Cash gave her a puzzled look, then turned his attention back to the street.

"Welcome home, Jason!" he hailed. Mankiller turned in his saddle at the sound of the greeting, waving but not stopping.

"I'll be by to see y'all directly," he called out, and Cash gave him another wave. The drifter noticed three workmen on ladders laboring to remove The Last Stand's sign from above the entrance: to repair or repaint it, he assumed.

He continued on past the saloon, heading toward a nice, respectable boarding house he remembered from his stay here some months earlier.

His time in Fort Rogers had been relatively short, but as he did in any town where he intended to stay more than a night, he had taken pains to thoroughly familiarize himself with its layout. More than once, this practice had saved him from being cornered in a blind alley.

Before he and his entourage reached the boarding house, another familiar voice called out his name, and this time he reined in. He smiled as he saw a game-legged man limping toward him as fast as he could manage.

"Hello, Corporal," he said in greeting.

Theo Hutton smiled broadly. He'd served under Mankiller during the recent unpleasantness, and owed him his life in more ways than one.

"I followed your advice, Sarge," he told Jason. "Moved the family here and set up my own tobacco shop. Doin' right well with it, too."

"Glad to hear it, Theo."

"I won't keep ya long, Sarge; but my wife Sally'd tan my hide if I didn't invite you home ta supper.

"At your convenience, of course," he added, eyeing the woman and child with his old comrade.

"I expect to be in town for at least a few days," Jason told him, "so I'd be glad to take you up on your offer. I'll get together with you soon."

"Sure thing. Good to see ya, Sarge."

"Good to see you too, Corporal."

Mankiller made no more stops before reaching his destination: a spacious, two-story house that was neatly maintained by a widow woman named Martha Pennington.

With Anita in his arms and Rosario beside him, Jason mounted the front steps of the house and knocked firmly on the door. The woman who opened it looked to be about fifty: with a face that might have been pretty in youth but now showed plainly the passing of each year since.

"What can I do for you?" she asked in clipped tones.

"We were wondering if you might have a vacancy," Jason explained. The woman eyed him suspiciously and sniffed.

"That depends," she said firmly. "I know who you are, mister—and I got no room for the likes of you."

Rosario gasped at this insult; Jason suppressed the desire to grin. This feisty old woman didn't quite reach the height of his chest and probably weighed less than a hundred pounds soaking wet: yet she showed no fear of him.

"Let's go, Jason," Rosario huffed. "I don't want to stay where my friends aren't welcome!"

"Hold on, now," the drifter said soothingly. "Let's not be hasty." Now he did smile at the scowling landlady.

"The room ain't for me, Miz Pennington. I'll make other arrangements for myself. I'm asking on behalf of these two young ladies."

Hearing that, Martha's demeanor softened: now she was smiling.

"Well, why didn't you say so?" she snorted, reaching out and snatching a startled Anita out of Mankiller's arms.

"I've got just the room for you, sweetie," she told the child, then turned her gaze to the mother. "But it'll cost you three dollars a week or ten dollars for the month—in advance. Meals are extra."

"Sounds fair," Jason said, reaching to dig some money out of his pants pocket, only to be stopped by Rosario.

"My friend here," she said, addressing the widow. "He'll be free to come and visit whenever he likes?"

"Well," Martha said warily, "I suppose. But not after ten o'clock. Nothing good ever happens after ten o'clock."

Jason again reached down into his pocket, and was again stopped by Rosario.

"It's my room," she insisted, "so I'll pay for it."

He knew that in addition to the remainder of the money he had given her months earlier, she also had the little she had made by selling her goats and chickens to a neighboring farmer before leaving home with him.

Appreciating her pride, he stuffed his own money back in his pocket as Rosario counted out ten dollars for Mrs. Pennington.

"After we unload your belongings," he told Rosario, "I mean to see about stabling my horse. While I'm at it, I'll try to sell the Indian pony. If you'd like, I can do likewise with your burro."

"That would be fine," she said. "I don't think I'll be needing him any more; I have a feeling we're here to stay."

Mankiller didn't tell her he meant to give her all of whatever he could get for the two beasts, knowing she would refuse to accept such an offer.

"Why don't you two come in and take a look at your new home," the widow Pennington said cheerfully as Jason began to unpack their belongings from the black pony.

He paused in untying the ropes when he heard Anita ask, "Will it be all right if Hector stays with us?"

"Why, sure it will, sweetie," Martha replied. "The place could use a good watchdog…to keep out the riff-raff!"

Jason, smiled, knowing the last comment was aimed at him, and resumed his unpacking.

CHAPTER 18

Mankiller left the livery stable with sixty more dollars in his pocket than when he had entered.

Besides selling the Indian pony and the burro, he'd also thrown in the slain outlaw's gun and saddle. The miscreant had not taken any better care of them than he had his horse.

The buckskin was essentially a sound mount, though, and Jason had decided to keep him; instructing the liveryman to brush him down good, fit him with new shoes and to mix generous portions of oats with his feed for the next few days.

He hadn't gone far from the stable, heading for his next business call, when a small boy came running up to him. This too presented a familiar face, and Jason nodded in greeting to the newsboy he knew only as Toby.

On his first stop in Fort Rogers, he bounty hunter had entered into a "business arrangement" with young Toby, whereby the newsboy promised to see to it that Jason always got a fresh copy of the local newspaper—the *Diligence*—whenever he was in town.

In truth, the arrangement had just been a ploy to get the stubbornly self-sufficient ten-year-old to accept some extra money Jason knew he, his mother and two younger sisters sorely needed.

"Hiya, Mr. Mankiller," the boy said cheerfully; his demeanor a far cry from the stoic, even suspicious face he had presented when first the drifter had met him.

"Hello, Toby." It seemed to please the lad that Jason had remembered his name.

"I didn't forget our deal," the boy said. "As soon as I heard you were back in town, I came runnin'." As proof, he proffered a copy of the newspaper, now nearly a week old.

"I knew I'd pardnered up with the right man," Jason told him. As was his habit, he gave the boy a nickel for the two-cent paper and told him to keep the change.

"Thanks," Toby chirped, pocketing the coin. "The next edition will be off the presses in a couple days."

"Good."

"I gotta go now," the newsie explained. "My maw's still havin' trouble findin' steady work, so I gotta hustle hard if I'm gonna help her keep food on the table." So saying, he spun and was off like a shot.

Smiling admiringly and shaking his head, Jason folded the newspaper in half and tucked it under his left arm before continuing onward.

His path took him past a wide, open lot where a handful of Mexican women were hard at work washing loads of laundry. He stopped here, scanning back and forth for one particular laundress. When he didn't see her, he approached the woman nearest to where he stood.

"Pardon me," he said in fluid Spanish. From the way the woman's eyes widened at the sight of him, he knew she had recognized him.

"When I was here earlier this year," he told her, "there was an old woman—a *vieja*—who worked here. Do you know her?"

"Yes."

"Do you know where she is?"

"I'm so sorry, senor," she replied. "But Sofia passed away just a few weeks after you left town." She reverently crossed herself as she conveyed the news to him.

"Oh. I'm sorry to hear that," Jason mumbled, at a loss for any other words. And the sentiment was real; though he had only a brief and passing acquaintance with the old woman. Until now, he had not even known her name.

By this time, several of the other laundresses had come over and were gathered around him.

"You should know, senor," the first woman told him, "that Sofia lived more comfortably in her last days because of the money you gave her."

"I'm glad to know that," he said.

Another woman now spoke. "A day seldom passed without Sofia talking about what a good and generous man you were."

"She asked us to pray for you," another woman offered. "And we do."

"Then I thank you all," he said, looking from one to another. "I 'spect I need all the prayers I can get."

"I tell you this, senor," the first woman declared. "Whenever you are here in town, and forever, you must bring your clothes to us to be cleaned. And there will be no charge for you."

The other women murmured their agreement.

Mankiller chuckled and looked down at the dirty, ragtag outfit he was currently wearing.

"I'm afeared most of these are gonna be consigned to the dustbin—except for this fine shirt that was a gift from a friend—just as soon as I'm able to acquire new duds.

"But as those need washing, you can rest assured that I'll be bringing 'em here to be cleaned." They all smiled at this.

"But you won't be doing it for free, ladies," he insisted. "I believe a body deserves fair wages for her labors."

They all smiled even more widely. One of them took his hand and kissed it.

He then bid the ladies farewell and continued on to the place that had initially been his destination: the First Cattlemen's Bank.

Upon entering the sedate establishment, Jason noted that the first teller to spy him in his wild appearance gave him a look of utter disdain. Then the officious little man apparently recognized the bounty hunter, for his expression quickly changed to one of respect (or, more likely, fear).

"Jason!"

The voice that called out a greeting to him was genuinely welcoming. It belonged to a man of about Mankiller's age, named Byron Longfellow (whose parents had obviously been of a literary bent). This young bank clerk had been so helpful to him before that Jason had made him his de facto business manager.

"Good to see you," Longfellow said, shaking the drifter's hand warmly and vigorously. "Come sit down."

The clerk led the way to his desk—which Jason approvingly noted was both larger and closer to the main office of the bank than had been the case previously.

"I'm sure you're busy," he told the clerk, who waved away any such consideration with a sweep of his hand, "so I'll get right down to brass tacks.

"First off: did all the money I been wiring to the bank since last I was here arrive all safe and sound?"

"Every penny," Longfellow assured him. "I keep your records right here in my desk, and you're encouraged to inspect them whenever you like."

"It won't hurt your feelings none if I do just that, will it?"

"Not at all. A smart man does keep close track of his assets." The clerk's expression grew more serious.

"From the amount and frequency of the deposits you've made—and even allowing that only half of the stories circulating about you are *true*—you've been a mighty busy man since I last saw you."

"I try not to stay idle too long."

"Well, if you don't mind me being totally frank, Jason—it doesn't look like you've come through the storm completely unscathed."

"We all get knocked around by life a bit, Byron—but in general, I'm well."

Longfellow knew better than to press the issue, so instead he slipped a ledger book out of a desk drawer and slid it across the desktop for Jason's inspection.

The banker grew concerned when he saw Mankiller frown after intensely studying the financial figures contained in the ledger.

"These numbers don't seem right," the bounty hunter said flatly and without inflection.

"Oh?" gulped Longfellow, growing more anxious as he leaned forward. "What's wrong with them?"

"Like you said," Jason told him, "I been depositing quite a bit. And I haven't been keeping a real close running tally of the amounts.

"But unless I forgot ever' bit of cipherin' my mama taught me, or the interest rates have shot up clear through the roof…I shouldn't have anywhere near this big a balance."

"Oh!" Byron gasped, visibly relieved. "Well, let me take a look, just to be sure." Now it was his turn to give the figures a serious study.

"Ah!" he said at last. "I think I see what has you confused. You didn't take into account the extra money you've earned from your share of Sam Dobbins' business."

"My share of what?" Jason said, now even more confused. "What are you talking about?"

"Of course," Longfellow said, the light of realization flaring in his eyes. "You wouldn't know."

"Know what?"

"Let me explain. After you left town back in the spring, Sam came to me with a proposition. He told me that just being your friend had been a big boon to him financially, and so he wanted to make you part owner of his business. He was quite insistent on it." Mankiller was frowning again, but Byron plunged ahead.

"I hope you'll recall that you gave me authority to act on your behalf and in your name where financial matters were concerned.

"This seemed like a wonderful opportunity—it only required a very small, very conservative outlay of cash on your part, and hardly any risk, really—so I agreed to it. I hope that's all right?"

"I s'pose," the drifter replied slowly, not at all convinced it was indeed all right.

"Looking at them numbers, The Last Stand must be doing right well for itself."

"Extremely well," Longfellow hastened to inform him. "As is the hotel."

"Hotel? Mebbe you'd better explain some more, Byron."

"Certainly. I'm sure you remember Bucktooth Bertha Hansen?"

"The madam who runs a house of ill repute over in the Tenderloin District?"

"The very same! Well, it seemed that after you paid a rather bloody house call on her establishment, Bertha lost her taste for running that sort of business.

"She was already…acquainted with Sam; so she approached him about buying the building from her. Sam then promptly closed it down, had some remodeling done—and re-opened at as a rather tony hotel. He let Bertha stay on to manage it."

"Well, I'll be damned," Jason whistled.

"It's done very good, very steady business thus far," Longfellow continued. "One room in particular is almost never vacant."

"Don't tell me," Mankiller practically moaned.

"You guessed it: the room where you gunned down the notorious outlaw Tyrone McClure!

"A steady stream of guests has been willing to pay double the going rate just to spend the night in that very chamber.

"Sam and Bertha even left the blood-stained original carpet in it when they renovated the rest of the structure."

Jason shook his head in bewilderment.

"Oh, and there's more to this story," Byron said conspiratorially, lowering his voice.

"Sam and Bertha have even begun to keep company together."

"No!" Jason exclaimed in feigned surprise.

"Yes!" Longfellow grinned. "It's pretty well known around town that the two of them are sweet on each other."

"That reminds me," Jason said. "When I left town before, you told me about a little gal who'd caught *your* eye. How's that progressing?"

Longfellow coughed uncomfortably. "It's not, I'm afraid. After I got to know her better, I realized she was a lot more interested in my position here at the bank and in the size of my own account than she was in me personally."

"That's too bad," Jason commiserated. "But if you're right, you're prob'ly better off without her.

"And a young fella like you, with your prospects—it won't take hardly no time a'tall for you to find someone more deserving of your affections."

"I suppose."

"Meanwhile," Jason went on, feeling it best to change the subject, "I got some more business I'd like to discuss with you, if you got the time."

"I always have time for you," Byron replied, relieved to drop the matter of his non-existent love life.

"I think I'd like to return Sam's favor," the drifter said, "by making him a pardner in any business ventures I might enter into in the future—not counting my bounty fees."

"I'm sure Sam would appreciate that," Longfellow nodded, beginning to scribble some notes as he listened.

"And I'd like you to be my pardner too, Byron."

"Me?"

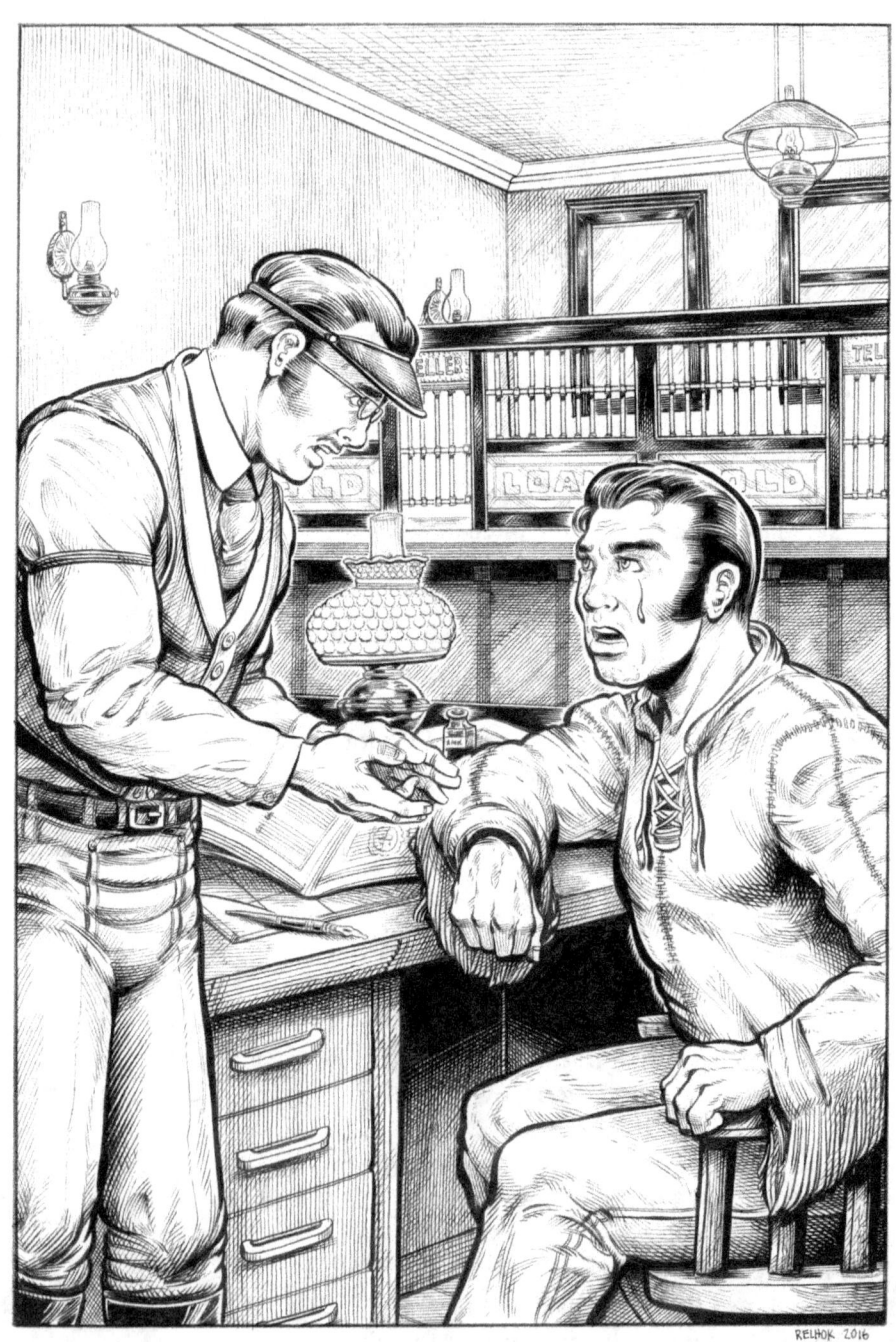

"We'll, I'll be damned."

"Sure. We can split everything even, three ways."

"No," Longfellow resisted. "That wouldn't be right. After all, initially at least, it would be mostly your money and entirely your reputation upon which the success of any such venture would depend."

"But it's what I want," Mankiller pressed. "And you and Sam will do plenty to earn whatever you get back."

"No; I still don't like it."

"I s'pect you can grow to like it."

The bank clerk sighed in exasperation. "You're not going to let this go, are you?"

"No, sir. I'm like a dog on a bone when I set my mind to somethin'."

Longfellow thought deeply for a minute before making further reply. "How about this? The three of us will form a partnership whereby you'll be entitled to seventy-five percent of any business profits." He quickly thrust up a hand to deter Jason from offering a fresh protest.

"Sam and I will manage and operate any such endeavors, and equally divide the other twenty-five percent. You're the one putting his life on the line to acquire our start-up capital, so that's good enough for me; and I have no doubt whatsoever that Sam will feel likewise." Longfellow now leaned back in his chair, folding his arms over his chest.

"Take it or leave it."

Mankiller scowled at the clerk to no effect. "Fine," he conceded. "We'll do it your way."

"Good! I'll arrange to have all the necessary paperwork for a partnership drawn up, and the three of us can sign it."

"Well, now that that's straightened out," the bounty hunter resumed, "I've got an idea that might be a good first venture for us."

"What might that be?"

Mankiller tapped the ledger now lying on the desktop between them. "Do I have enough money to purchase a few parcels of land hereabouts?"

Longfellow chuckled. "Jason, you've got enough money to buy half the county if you want! What did you have in mind?"

"The first parcel would be for me personal. You know that little crick running just to the north of town?"

"Contrary Creek?"

"If that's what it's called. Why is it called that?"

"Because, unlike most such little streams in this part of Texas, it never runs completely dry, even in the hottest summer."

"Well, I want a piece of land alongside it. Don't have to be much: no more'n an acre or two. I'll point out the exact spot to you later."

"All right."

"And now we get down to real business."

In short, terse terms, Mankiller told the clerk about his chance meeting with the surveyor Lee Burris—and of how Burris had chosen to repay the bounty hunter for his kindness.

"Turns out, Mr. Burris was the lead man for a team of surveyors in the employ of the *Louisiana-Texas Western Railway Company*. Their job was to map out the next stretch the railroad would take outta Dallas.

"According to Burris, one section of that line is gonna run right straight along the southern outskirts of Fort Rogers. He sorta told me this on the sly; no one else knows about it yet."

Longfellow sat up straighter as he immediately realized the possible implications of this bit of confidential information.

"Good Lord," he whispered. "The price of land around here is still depressed. If we buy up tracts of land along the planned railroad route at today's bargain rates –"

"We'll soon be able to re-sell it for two or three times what we paid for it," Mankiller finished for him.

"Maybe more," Byron said. "This is incredible. "I'll get to work on buying up parcels of land as quick as I can.

"Discretely, of course," he added.

"I figgered you'd prob'ly be good at that," Mankiller said.

"I'll keep you updated every step of the way," Longfellow promised. "Was there any other pressing business you needed to discuss with me?"

"Mebbe. There used to be a nice little cantina here, on the west end of town."

"Francisco's. I know it well."

"I ate there several times myself," Jason told him. "Liked it real well. But when I rode inta town a little while ago, I noticed it was boarded up.

"Do you know why it went outta business?"

"It wasn't because it failed," Longfellow explained. "It had a very good, very loyal clientele. But apparently some sort of crisis below the border caused Francisco to close down the cantina, pack up his family and return to Mexico."

"That's too bad," Jason said. But inside he was thinking of a simple truth: that, generally speaking, nothing is so bad that it isn't good for somebody else.

"Let me float another idea past you," he said to Byron, with that thought in mind.

This last order of business took but a few minutes to conclude, and the drifter rose to take his leave; giving Longfellow a firm handshake before exiting the bank.

He pulled up short as he stepped through its door, only mildly surprised when he saw the man leaning against the bank's hitching post, glaring at him.

"I been lookin' for you, Mankiller," Marshal Clayton Russell growled.

CHAPTER 19

"If you hadn't come lookin' for me, Marshal," Mankiller said to Russell, "I'da come lookin' for you." He immediately saw that the lawman's frame was a bit leaner and tougher looking than he remembered. And there was more steel in the graying man's eyes than when first they'd met.

"You here on the trail of a wanted man?" Russell wasted no time in asking.

"Nope. Just here to take care of a little business and to rest up for a spell."

"'Pears like you need to," the lawman said bluntly. "You look as bad as a barber's cat."

"I been better," Jason conceded. "How are things around here?"

"Busy," Russell told him. "At least partly due to you," he contended.

"How's that?"

"We got more people here now, 'cause of you. Some for the better: like Theo Hutton and some other new arrivals who apparently came here at your suggestion.

"Some not so good. The notoriety you brought to Fort Rogers with your multiple killings has also attracted a bunch of undesirables. The Tenderloin has expanded considerably."

Mankiller knew from before that the Tenderloin was the name the locals had given to the east end of town: the red light district.

It held half a dozen brothels—including, rumor had it, one with young male prostitutes—and an opium den. An underground arena used for cock and dog fights as well as human bare-knuckle brawls. The seedier class of saloons.

The western boundary of the Tenderloin, Fifth Street, running north and south, was known as the Dragline. As long as the purveyors of the worst forms of vice remained east of the Line, the rest of the town usually tolerated them. Even the law ignored it—but only up to a point.

"Because of its expansion," Marshal Russell explained to Mankiller, "and the kind of disorderly conduct it encourages, I've had to hire on additional deputies.

"Which means you're also making more money now," Jason said.

"How's that?"

"You're imposing more fines, ain'tcha? For disturbing the peace, offending public decency?"

"Oh, hell yeah. Lots more."

"Well, don't you get a share of that revenue?"

"I got no idea what you're talking about, bounty hunter." Jason could tell by Russell's expression that the lawman was speaking truthfully.

"Let me explain it to you, Marshal," he said. "Ever' lawman I've ever had more than a nodding acquaintance with had at least two different sources of income: his regular monthly salary and a percentage of all the fines levied from lawbreakers, and licensing fees from saloons, whorehouses and the like."

Jason didn't mention that many of these badge toters had yet a third source of income, derived from owning a piece of the action at those selfsame saloons and cathouses. He didn't figure Russell to be the sort to engage in any such activity.

"Are you tellin' me true, Mankiller?"

"I am."

"I didn't know," the lawman mumbled, clearly embarrassed to admit to his ignorance of any such practice.

"I mostly worked as a drover before pinning on a badge here. Nobody else ever mentioned such a thing before now."

"Of course not," Jason said with heartfelt disgust. "They've been depositing all you put your life on the line to collect into the town treasury—after skimming a little off the top for themselves, I'd wager."

"The bastards!" Russell hissed. "I wouldn't put that past a damned one of 'em!"

"Calm down, Russell. Don't get all riled up," the drifter counseled. "I suggest you just take up the matter with the Mayor and the City Council first chance you get. You might even try dropping my name into the conversation."

"What do you mean?" The lawman was now hanging onto Jason's every word.

"Just tell 'em that if you're gonna have to deal with the likes o' *me* on a regular basis from now on, they got to give you a raise in salary—or else, say, twenty-five percent of all the fees and fines you collect for the city.

"Chances are they'll agree to that rather than pony up a higher salary outta their own coffers." As he finished speaking, he saw Russell's head bobbing up and down slightly.

"I thank you for the advice," the lawman said.

"My pleasure, Marshal. There's one more thing. If you don't have a written contract with the city, stipulating to all these terms and saying that you're entitled to a pension when your law days is done—well, sir, you oughtta get one.

"Tell you what you do, Russell. Go on into the bank and speak with a fella there by the name of Byron Longfellow. Ask him to recommend a good lawyer who'll represent you and help negotiate a contract.

"Just tell Byron I sent you."

"I'll do that," Russell declared emphatically.

"Are you in trouble with the law already, ya mangy miscreant?"

Both Mankiller and Russell turned at the sound of this new voice to see Sam Dobbins, smiling exuberantly. So happy was he that he actually threw his arms around Jason, ignoring the drifter's discomfort as he hugged him.

"C'mon," the saloonkeeper said, slinging a paternal arm around Jason's shoulders. "I got a lot to tell ya; a lot to show ya!"

"Are we done, Marshal?" Jason asked of Russell.

"For now, yeah. Just watch your step." The lawman's voice was still gruff, but his features had softened.

Clearly, he appreciated all that Mankiller had told him. For a moment, it looked as if he might even extend a handshake to the drifter; but instead he thrust both hands in his pockets and sauntered past them, heading into the bank.

"Drop into my place later, Clay," Dobbins said magnanimously. "You know the first drink's always on the house for peace officers!"

From the front window of a nearby building, a tall, thin, balding man named Ezra Vail stood and watched all that had transpired.

One look at his face would clearly reveal that he was not happy that Jason Mankiller had returned to Fort Rogers.

CHAPTER 20

As they walked down the street together, Jason tried to be stern with the saloonkeeper.

"I gotta tell ya, Sam," he scolded, "I ain't happy about you goin' behind my back and making business deals with young Longfellow."

"You ain't really mad at me, are ya?" Dobbins asked.

"Well, not mad exactly—"

"Then get glad!" the saloonkeeper fairly bubbled. "Trust me, if you ain't already—you will be by the time I show you our new enterprises!" He motioned out over the city ahead of them.

"It's helped a lot that things in general have gotten better since you first came here: we got new people, new businesses. The two go hand in glove.

"Granted, we haven't completely shook off the effects of the Depression; that's true most everywhere, from what I hear. But things are definitely on the upswing."

"Glad to hear that."

"You should be. Since the improvements more or less coincided with you coming to town and putting Fort Rogers on the map—some folks here have started thinking of you sort of like a good luck charm!"

"Not ever'one would agree with that sentiment," Mankiller said, thinking specifically of the marshal.

"Aw, there's always gonna be a few naysayers," Sam replied. "Pay 'em no mind: I don't. Ah—here we are."

Jason found they were now standing directly outside the entrance of the former cathouse turned hotel. He smiled at the large sign over the entrance proclaiming it now to be called the *Hansen House*.

Following Dobbins inside, he immediately saw that the place had undergone a complete transformation since last he's seen it; it was now cleaner, brighter, airier, better smelling and not nearly so gaudy in its décor.

Everything seemed downright tasteful.

He quickly saw that the plump, middle-aged mistress of the house had been the object of an equally striking metamorphosis. Bertha Hansen, who seemed to be giving instructions to a bellboy, was dressed demurely in a nice dress that covered her from her round chin to her ankles. While still wearing a little make-up, in vanity's effort to conceal her age, she no longer looked like the painted cat of his earlier acquaintance.

Spying Sam Dobbins, Bertha's not-unattractive face lit up, and she rushed over to give him a welcoming hug and a chaste kiss on the cheek.

When she swiveled at the hips and saw Jason, however, the smile disappeared and her face blanched with fear. But only until the bounty hunter greeted her.

"Hello, Miz Bertha," he said. Smiling, he took her hand and graciously bowed to kiss it lightly, whereupon she giggled like a schoolgirl.

"Is everything all right, ma'am?" a deep voice inquired.

Seemingly from nowhere, a towering black man was now standing beside them. With his muscular frame and shaved head, he looked rather incongruous in a tight-fitting formal suit and tie. It was obvious that the cellophane collar of his shirt was straining to encompass the thickness of his neck.

"Everything's fine, Caesar," Bertha replied, patting the arm of the loyal and formidable man who had been the head bouncer at her old business.

"Caesar's the hotel's concierge," Dobbins explained.

"If that word means 'giant,' he sure fills the bill," Jason deadpanned.

"You must check out our dining room, Mr. Mankiller," Bertha gushed, lacing her arms through those of both Jason and Sam and steering them away from the glowering Caesar.

Jason was impressed by what they had done with what before had simply been the front parlor of Bertha's cathouse. It had not only been remodeled but also expanded into what had the appearance of a fairly elegant restaurant.

"What do you think?" Bertha asked hopefully.

"Mighty nice, ma'am," Jason replied. "And clearly it's doing great business."

"That's because it's patronized by townspeople as well as hotel guests," she explained. "We make sure to provide good food and good service, and it pays off well."

"I'll leave it in your capable hands, pigeon," Sam said, giving Bertha a peck on the cheek. "I have more I want Jason to see."

"You'll be back in time for us to have supper together?"

"You know I will, if I can."

"You and Bertha have done a good job, Sam," Jason said as the two men left the hotel.

"She's proved to be a good partner."

"In more ways than one, I take it."

Dobbins colored slightly. "She's a good woman, Jason."

"I'm sure she is."

"It's not good for a man to be all alone. That's something you should think about and take to heart."

"Yes, papa," the drifter teased. "I got a question about your hotel, though."

"*Our* hotel."

"Right. It's mighty nice, all right; just like I said. Maybe *too* nice—for a place in the Tenderloin, I mean."

"That's a good point," Dobbins agreed. "The thing is, technically speaking, the Hansen House isn't in the Tenderloin District."

"Oh? How's that?"

"I'm sure as we approached the hotel that you saw all the construction work being done on either side of it to the north and south."

"Sure."

"That's all ours, too."

"The devil you say."

"I do. After Byron—acting on your behalf, of course—and me bought Bertha's whorehouse, we snatched up all these other lots as well. Got 'em for a song, given the location.

"Behind the hotel, just to the east, were several properties that had been abandoned and allowed to fall into ruin.

"We bought those even cheaper, razed every rat's den there to the ground and had a park built in their place.

"It's open to everyone in the city and draws a good crowd during the day. Best of all, it acts as a sort of buffer between the Tenderloin proper and the rest of Fort Rogers."

"But Marshal Russell told me the Tenderloin has been growing too," Jason said.

"And he didn't lie," Sam replied. "Though I wouldn't be surprised if he exaggerated a bit. But all its growth has been farther to the east, away from us. And its patrons mostly keep the peace, by keeping their meanness in their own area and steering clear of the nice part of town.

"Partly, their propriety in such is due to an increased presence on the streets by Russell and his deputies.

"But I think that, even more so, they're kept in line by the knowledge that Jason Mankiller would not take kindly to any damages wrought by unwarranted incursions from the Tenderloin."

"Glad I could be of help," Jason said dryly. "I was beginning to think you and Byron didn't need me a'tall."

"Oh, no. It's *all* you, son," Sam said earnestly. "Whether you know it or not, you're what sparked me to expand my horizons.

"And whether you're here in person or not, it's your presence that drives every bit of it."

The drifter didn't know how to reply to that, so he said nothing.

"Ah! Here's our real gem," Dobbins said proudly, gesturing toward a large building just a few doors down from the Hansen House. A wide sign over its entrance identified it as the *Grand Comique*. From inside could be heard the distinctive sounds of carpenters at work.

"A theater?" Jason asked.

"A dee-luxe one!" Sam beamed. "Like I said, things are picking up for most folks around here. And once people get a little extra money in their pockets—they'll look to spend some of it on being entertained in one way or another.

"It's designed to host all kinds of acts: everything from burlesque to Shakespeare. We've already scheduled it8s Grand Opening for a few days from now, and booked Eddie Foy himself as the headliner!"

"You've gotten right ambitious since I left town," Mankiller cautioned. "I just hope your eyes ain't bigger than your belly."

"I don't think they are, Jason. I really don't. Me and Byron hope to fill the rest of this block with tenants ranging from retail stores to more restaurants. Potential tenants have already started making inquiries; a new billiard parlor should be up and running soon.

"What we're doing is re-shaping the face of Fort Rogers: me, Byron and you."

"I never thought of myself as a town builder," the drifter muttered.

"That's 'cause you underestimate your potential, Jason," Sam said, slapping him on the back.

"Now what say we head back to my place for a drink?"

As they neared Dobbins' saloon, Mankiller pulled up short, his face darkly clouding over. Only now had he been able to see that the old sign he thought was simply being repaired had in fact been totally replaced.

The new sign that now occupied the space above the front doors bore the name *The Bloody Eye*. Below the name was prominently displayed a depiction of a large eye appearing to shed a red tear of blood.

"You've gone way too far now, Sam," the bounty hunter snarled, clearly appalled by the signage. "Take it down."

"Don't get upset," Dobbins urged, trying to mollify his already reluctant partner.

"A lot of our customers had already started calling the old place by that name anyway; so I just figured I'd make it official."

"I don't like the look of it," Mankiller persisted.

"Think of it like a tribute," the saloonkeeper said, grasping for words. "Plus...it'll draw in even more business." In reply, the drifter fixed him with a baleful stare that made his mouth run dry.

"If anybody else had done this, Sam—I'da horsewhipped 'im."

"Give it a chance, Jason. I promise I won't let anybody disrespect the name *or* you."

Mankiller looked up at the sign, shaking his head.

"Don't ever make me regret letting you do this."

"I won't, son. Swear to God."

Walking up the steps to the sidewalk and then pushing his way through the batwing doors, Jason saw that the saloon had been renovated nearly as much as had Bertha Hansen's whorehouse.

A new, shiny mahogany bar ran for fifty feet down one side of the structure; the entire length of wall behind it sparkled with large mirrors, spaced along either side of two garish paintings of reclining nude women. The candles of an enormous, three-tiered chandelier hanging from the ceiling cast a soft glow over the entire place.

"I'll give you this, Sam," Jason said. "You've turned the old place inta a real stem-winder."

"Ain't I, though?"

Back in one corner, a short man was tickling the ivories of an upright piano. Against the rear wall stood the small raised platform where Mankiller had sat and kept guard over the saloon for a brief time during his first stay in Fort Rogers. Sam Dobbins pointed to it.

"We keep it empty now," he told Jason, "except when someone pays twenty-five cents to sit there and hold your sawed-off shotgun for two minutes."

"You're still finding suckers willing to do that?"

"Plenty of 'em. And for fifty cents more they can have a picture taken there."

Jason assumed the place hadn't become completely civilized since his last visit. Just a few feet away from where he had perched, an identical second platform had been erected; manning it was a stocky fellow clearly capable of maintaining order.

Mankiller also saw four or five scantily clad girls—clearly soiled doves— flitting from patron to patron, hustling for drinks and more.

When one of them sashayed past Jason, giving him a wink and what she hoped was a seductive smile, he cast an inquisitive look at Dobbins.

"What?" Sam said, smiling wolfishly. "Bertha gave up that business— not me!"

From the moment he'd stepped through the swinging doors of the saloon, Jason's eyes had been searching for Jane Starr, and he quickly spied her at her faro table. When she glanced up, he caught her eye, smiling and waving to her.

To his disappointment, she did no more than return a slight nod of her head before turning her attention back to the game at hand.

Puzzled by her rather cool response to him, Mankiller started to move toward her—only to be intercepted by a very jovial Cash Carpenter.

"About time you got here, Jason!" the gambler said, taking him by the arm and pulling him over to the bar.

"I'll have a champagne flip, Trey," Cash told the bartender. "And for my friend," he looked to the bounty hunter. "Name your poison, Jason. On me."

Mankiller smiled at Carpenter. "Coffee'll do just fine for me, Cash. I ain't had any in awhile."

"I'll join you," Sam Dobbins said, moving around to the opposite side of the bar. The help knew to keep a fresh pot of the brew on hand for the bar owner's pleasure, and he now poured two cups.

As he turned and set one of the cups in front of Mankiller, his gaze flicked toward the door and he scowled.

"Damn."

"What is it, Sam?" Jason asked.

"Trouble."

CHAPTER 21

Mankiller pivoted slowly, following the saloonkeeper's gaze to the bar's batwing doors.

Standing there was what could only be described as a bear of a man: standing at least six-feet three-inches in height and carrying well over two hundred pounds of what appeared to be mostly muscle. He had an unruly head of rust colored hair atop his head and sported a bushy moustache of the same color. He planted himself just inside the doorway as if posing. His clenched fists were on his hips and he appeared to be swaying slightly.

"Who is he?" Jason inquired softly.

"His name's Dick Johnson," Sam replied, "but most everybody calls him *Copperhead.*"

"What's his story?"

"I told you things have improved mightily around here, and they have. But work prospects are still a little tight; especially for a man with no education and few job skills, like Dick there."

"That's too bad."

"Yeah. He's been scouring the market for weeks now, with no luck. Lately, he's taken to trying to salve his frustration with drink.

"Enough drinks and he becomes real belligerent. Then he's mean as a meat ax."

On this day, Copperhead appeared already to be well into his cups as he bellied up to the bar just a couple feet away from Mankiller and loudly ordered a beer. When it came, he nearly drained the mug in a single deep swallow.

"Say," he mumbled, glancing over and seeing the distinctive tattoo on Jason's left cheek, "Yer that Mankiller feller, ain'tcha?"

"I am," the drifter replied without favoring the drunk with so much as a sideways glance.

"That's hard ta believe," Copperhead said, his speech noticeably slurred. "Why, from the stories I heard tell around here, I expected you'd be ten feet tall and broad as an ox yoke!"

Jason smiled at him tightly. "Yeah, well, you know how people like to stretch the truth some times."

"Stretched, hell—it's been strung out clear to the county line! You don't look tough enough ta shoo flies off a gut bucket!"

"You might be right, pilgrim," Jason said amiably, while inside he fought to hold down the anger he was beginning to feel toward this insulting drunkard.

"Just pull in your horns, Dick," Sam Dobbins advised quietly. "Don't nobody want no trouble today."

"Mebbe *I* do, bar dog!" Copperhead snarled.

"Well, I'll tell you, boy—you got the wrong pig by the tail if you try to crawl this man's hump," Dobbins declared.

"Keep yer mouth shut!" Johnson snapped, reaching across to grasp the front of Sam's shirt and yank him nearly over the bar.

"And you keep your hands to yourself, mister," Mankiller said, grabbing the big man's wrist in a deceptively powerful grip.

Johnson's eyes narrowed in a bloody rage, but Jason tried one more time to keep the situation from escalating out of control.

"Why don't you let me buy you a fresh drink?" he said, forcing a smile to his lips. His offer had the opposite of its desired effect.

"Yer the real tall hog at the trough in these parts, ain'tcha?" Copperhead said with disdain.

"Well, the rest o' this town might be grateful for the table scraps yer willin' ta throw their way—but I don't kow-tow ta any stinkin' bounty killer.

"And I won't have one lay his hands on me!"

With surprising speed, Copperhead released Sam's shirt, pulled free of Jason's grasp—and then hit the drifter across the mouth with a sweeping backhand blow.

Without conscious thought, Mankiller's right hand flashed across his body to his cross-draw holster, grabbing the butt of his .44 caliber Colt. He had the revolver drawn, cocked and aimed by the time Sam Dobbins realized he was about to witness a killing at close hand.

"I ain't heeled!" Copperhead bellowed loudly, throwing his empty hands up in the air.

"Then get heeled, you sonuvabitch!" Mankiller barked, tasting his own blood in his mouth.

The harrowing events of the past week had left his nerves on the razor's edge, and he was in no mood to be pushed.

Still, such was his self-control that he slowly lowered the hammer on his pistol and returned it to its holster.

Seeing he was in no immediate danger, Copperhead Johnson smiled; actually, it was more of a sneer.

"Sam," Jason said to the saloonkeeper in a voice made even more menacing by its steady softness, "give 'im a gun."

"Don't bother, bar dog," Johnson said smugly, lowering his hands and hooking his thumbs in the waist of his trousers.

"Everybody knows you can't be beat with a pistol, gun slick," he challenged. "But how big a man are ya *without* a gun?"

"Big enough to plow you under like last year's chaff," Jason growled, reaching for the buckle of his gunbelt.

From behind, Cash Carpenter put a restraining hand on Mankiller's shoulder. "You can't fight him with your bare hands, Jason," he urgently whispered into the drifter's ear.

"He's got at least fifty pounds on you, man," the gambler warned. "And he's rumored to have killed more than one man with those ham-sized fists of his!"

Mankiller hesitated for a heartbeat, letting his gaze peripherally scan the saloon. He could tell that all eyes were on him: expectantly waiting to see if he would accept the challenge or back down.

He removed his gunbelt and set it atop the bar.

"Here, now," Sam said, and both of the would-be combatants turned to see the saloonkeeper had produced a shotgun from underneath the bar and was now holding it on them.

"I ain't heeled!"

"There'll be no unrestrained fisticuffs in my fine place," Dobbins firmly declared

Jason heard a familiar cocking sound that told him the shotgun guard at the back of the saloon had also swung his weapon in their direction as he descended from his perch and moved toward them.

Then Sam smiled slightly and jerked his head in the direction of the joint's back wall.

"Take it out to the *bullpen*, boys!" he shouted.

CHAPTER 22

A chorus of cheers erupted from the patrons of the bar.

Many saloons on the frontier had a "bullpen;" usually just a small, bare back room where those too drunk to walk or crawl home unassisted could be dumped to sleep it off on the floor.

But such rooms were also used to play host to fights such as the one now brewing between Mankiller and Copperhead Johnson.

At the moment, it only being late afternoon, only one bar patron was occupying the bullpen floor. Multiple hands roughly grabbed him by the collar and the seat of his pants and threw him out of the room.

It proved fortunate that Sam Dobbins had made his bullpen larger than most: else it wouldn't have held the sized crowd that began to push and shove its way in. As if word had miraculously spread, men had even come rushing in from out on the streets to bear witness. No one wanted to miss seeing what was bound to be an epic battle, the details of which would doubtless be long and oft repeated. In time to come, twice as many would falsely claim to have been there than actually were present the day of the big brawl.

Unnoticed by Mankiller or anyone else, Jane Starr had positioned herself at the back of the throng, anxiously looking on.

Having made his abortive effort to prevent this fight, the gaming man inside Cash Carpenter came to the forefront and decided he might as well exploit it.

"Place your bets, gentlemen," he cried, walking around the naturally forming circle of bystanders. "I'm giving two-to-one odds," he loudly proclaimed, "in favor of Copperhead Johnson!"

Hearing this, Mankiller fixed the gambler with a wondering look.

Cash merely shrugged, grinned crookedly and winked: as if to silently say, "business is business."

Jason pulled his prized Indian tunic off over his head and tossed it to one of the spectators for safekeeping.

As the last of the bar denizens crammed into the bullpen, Sam Dobbins drew close to Cash.

"How's the wagering going?" he asked.

"Brisk," Carpenter replied cheerfully. "And even at two-to-one, most of the money's on Copperhead!"

"We'll see about that," Sam said. "Someone close the door!" he shouted a few moments later, and heard it slam shut.

The only people left outside the confines of the bullpen were the bartenders and the shotgun guard. Even the soiled doves were all inside to watch the fight; they knew a good, brutal brawl would heat up the blood of every man there and thus increase their prurient business later.

"Give 'em room, boys! Give 'em room!" Sam shouted, pushing the crowd back away from the combatants as far as the walls of the enclosure would allow.

Dobbins then stepped between Mankiller and Johnson, asserting his authority in his position of self-appointed referee.

"Are there to be any rules?" he asked of both of them.

"Just one," Copperhead declared fiercely. "We don't stop till one of us can't stand no more!"

Sam looked at Jason to see if this was acceptable to him, and the drifter nodded.

"Ready?" Sam said, holding his right arm out between the two of them before jerking it away. "Go!"

The battle that followed was one that would go down in the annals of the history of Fort Rogers, Texas.

At first, Mankiller was able to use his greater speed to his advantage. His head bobbed and weaved away from punches; he danced lightly back and forth on the balls of his feet. Between moves, his own fists flicked out, connecting with jabs and blows to the body.

But though his punches were landing, they seemed to be having little effect on the walking slab of beef that was Copperhead Johnson, and failed to put him down.

Nor did Johnson fail to connect occasionally, with each blow that did so landing like a slap from a sock filled with coins.

Jason landed a straight jab that flattened his opponent's nose and drew blood, but he paid for it by taking a roundhouse to the side of the head that left his skull ringing.

Worse, he was growing more tired with each passing minute, slowing down as his arms and legs grew heavier. His many recent injuries and lack of sufficient time to rest and recover fully were beginning to take their toll. As he slowed, he began to take more punishment from his larger opponent.

A slashing roundhouse right opened a gash above Mankiller's left eye and dropped him to his knees. The crowd roared in anticipation.

"The books are closed!" Cash Carpenter yelled, as onlookers tried to place final bets in favor of Copperhead now that the end seemed certain.

Swiping the blood from his eye as he struggled to rise, Jason saw Johnson rushing forward to finish him off.

Mankiller's right fist shot straight forward, catching Copperhead in his midsection and stopping him in his tracks. The drifter rose swiftly from his knees, using the momentum to deliver an uppercut that rocked Johnson backwards.

For an interminable period of time, the two fighters stood toe-to-toe, exchanging savage blows. Each began to bleed from multiple lacerations: their punches sending sprays of gore into the faces of the nearest onlookers. It seemed to drive the bar patrons to an even greater frenzy.

Cash Carpenter took time to snatch a brief glimpse at his pocket watch, frowning as he did so. The slugfest had been going for nearly an hour now, with no rest periods. He wondered how much longer his friend could last.

He grimaced and groaned as, as if in answer to his unspoken question, Mankiller took a solid shot straight to the middle of his face. Spectators pressed aside as he staggered backwards and slammed into a wall. Clearly reeling, he sagged against the wall, his hands and head lowered.

Seeing the opening he had been awaiting, Copperhead recklessly lunged forward with both arms extended straight ahead. He meant to get his huge hands around Mankiller's throat and throttle him into submission—or death.

Instead, he discovered too late that his rash attack had left him open to a counterstrike: just as Mankiller had desperately hoped. The drifter pushed away from the wall at the last possible instant, so as to slide between Copperhead's out-thrust arms. He then delivered a short, chopping blow to the big man's throat, using the edge of one hand.

Suddenly unable to breathe, choking and experiencing searing pain, Copperhead gripped at his neck with both hands. Stumbling back, he bent over double as he struggled to suck air down his damaged windpipe.

Jason grabbed Copperhead by the back of his shirt, spun him twice and slammed him headfirst into the wall. With a sickening crunch, the big man's crown split and began to gush blood down his face.

Mankiller turned him again, slammed him back against the wall. He punched the big man in the belly, then straightened him with a vicious uppercut.

Now it was Copperhead's arms that hung uselessly at his sides as Jason began to pummel him with blow after savage blow, snapping his head sharply from side to side.

"That's enough, son!" Sam Dobbins yelled, throwing his arms around Mankiller from behind and pulling him away from the insensate Copperhead.

"He'll fall, if you just give 'im the chance!"

Indeed, without Jason holding him up, Johnson slid down the wall to his knees, then pitched forward face down with such force as to make the floorboards vibrate.

"You did it!" Sam shouted wildly, spinning the stunned Jason around to face him. As the room swelled with a cacophony of cheers and boos, Mankiller's eyes fluttered upward and he began to topple over backwards.

But several sets of hands reached out to stop his fall, clutching at him as the spectators practically carried him out of the bullpen and back into the main chamber of the saloon. Now all were cheering him like he was a triumphant gladiator in the ancient Roman coliseum.

No one gave another thought to Copperhead Dick Johnson, left alone and unconscious on the bullpen floor.

As he re-entered the saloon proper, Jason again sought out Jane. He saw her sitting at her table, back to him, calmly playing a game of solitaire as she waited for her faro players to return.

Mankiller would never know that she had witnessed the entire fight; nor know of the emotional torment that his physical pain had caused her.

As Jason was dragged along back to the bar and sagged against it, Sam Dobbins went around it, headed for the coffeepot. To his surprise, Mankiller shook his head.

"Gimme a double shot of the worst Kansas sheep dip you got, Sam."

Dobbins was concerned by this request, for he knew the drifter never partook of anything stronger than beer; and that only sparingly. Since the night, years earlier, in the aftermath of the Battle of Gettysburg, when he had allowed himself, in a drunken stupor, to be tattooed with the blood red teardrop on his cheek, he had been a virtual tea-totaler.

Then the saloonkeeper saw his young friend work his tongue around inside his mouth and spit out a bloody tooth.

"For strictly medicinal purposes," Jason told him, smiling weakly.

Sam obliged, filling a large shot glass with the cheapest, foulest snakehead whiskey in stock. Mankiller knocked back the entire glass in a single gulp. He swished it around his mouth, grimacing as the alcohol sharply stung the bleeding abrasions inside and on his lips—then unceremoniously spit it out into a nearby cuspidor.

"Now chase it down with this," Sam said, sliding a cup of pitch-black coffee toward him. "It'll do ya good; it's thick enough to float a colt."

"Thanks," Jason gasped, wincing only slightly as he sipped the strong brew. "I'm sorry if I caused you and yer business any undue hardship, pardner."

Sam brushed the words aside with a flick of a hand. "Pshaw. Why, hell, boy—even when you're causing trouble you're making me money!"

The comment puzzled Mankiller, until he saw Sam pull a thick roll of cash out of his vest pocket and wink at the drifter.

"You don't think I'd ever bet *against* you, do you, son?"

Cash Carpenter elbowed his way through the crowd pressing around Mankiller and gave the bounty hunter a hearty slap on the back, causing his knees to nearly buckle under him.

"There's my hero," he told Jason. "Even after paying off the few brave souls who dared to bet on you," he nodded toward Sam, "I came away with a hefty bankroll!"

"I'm tickled for ya," Jason drawled.

"Yes, indeed," Cash went on, ignoring the sarcasm, "it was a battle for the ages. The two of you fought like a pair of Kilkenny cats."

"Yeah," Sam laughed, "till Jason here knocked ol' Copperhead galley west!"

As the crowd roared, the drifter waved for Sam to lean in closer.

"I got an idea I'd like to share," he told the saloonkeeper. "I been thinking about it ever since you told me about that nice little park you built on the edge of the Tenderloin."

"What about it?"

"Well, I like the thought of it: at least in principal. But it occurred to me that such a place could become less of a paradise after the sun goes down."

Dobbins frowned slightly and nodded. "To be honest, Jason, I have heard stories about a few unsavory characters and their activities there after dark."

"Daylight or dark," Mankiller asserted, "that's the kind of thing that could spill over into the area you're developing and throw a real squirrel in the works."

"I take it you got a notion on how to prevent that from happening?"

"Mebbe. It seems to me that it might be money well spent to have your own security force; just three or four men to patrol the park and the surroundings, at least at night. More if needed. To keep the undesirables away from your—from *our* hotel and theater."

"I think you may be right, son."

"And if you're bound and determined to make me a part of this venture, we might as well go whole hog.

"Spread the word through the Tenderloin that Jason Mankiller has personally declared the park and all points west of it to be off-limits—and that violations won't be tolerated."

Sam smiled broadly. This was exactly the sort of thing he had been hoping for from the bounty hunter. The kind of reputation Jason had built for himself was a great deterrent to most troublemakers.

"And I'm thinking," Mankiller continued, "that Copperhead Johnson might be a good choice to head up our little security force."

"For real?" Sam said, not sure he'd heard correctly.

"Sure. He's tough as nails, and ain't got sense enough to be afraid," Jason said. "So why not? Provided he pledges to stay off the bottle, o' course."

Dobbins studied the drifter's face to make sure he was serious, then shrugged. "All right. I'll talk the matter over with him personal-like, m'boy," the saloonkeeper pledged, then raised his voice.

"Just as soon as he *wakes up!*"

The bar patrons clustered about joined him in laughing, though many of them didn't know why; and rounds of drinks began to be ordered by various and sundry.

The wily Dobbins noticed that Mankiller graciously accepted every drink that was thrust upon him by an admirer, raising his glass in a toast to the benefactor—then surreptitiously slid the glass down the bar, knowing it would be eagerly snatched up and disposed of by someone else.

Finally, having endured all the glad-handing he could bear, Mankiller leaned over the bar to catch Dobbins' ear.

"Do you still have a room upstairs you can spare?" he asked the saloonkeeper. "I could sure use a place to lay down and rest for a spell."

"Sure!" Sam told him. "Go on up. It's the same room you stayed in before; it's sorta permanently reserved for you. I had one of the girls go up and air it out a little as soon as I seen you was back in town!"

"Thanks, Sam. I'm obliged."

As soon as he was able to push away from the bar and through the throng surrounding it, Jason again sought out Jane Starr. Again, though, she seemed to have eyes only for her faro layout.

Too tired and weak and disinclined to try to interrupt her at her work, the drifter walked on by and headed up the stairs.

Halfway up, Mankiller's feet became so heavy he could barely lift them. He tripped on a step, pitching forward heavily onto his hands and knees.

He stayed in that position, his vision blurring, until he felt gentle hands grabbing and steadying him.

Jason lifted his head to see Jane kneeling beside him, a fearful expression twisting her lovely features.

"Must be gettin' clumsy in my old age," he jested—then slumped forward, unconscious.

CHAPTER 23

The following day, in her new quarters at Mrs. Pennington's boarding-house, Rosario Mendoza swayed back and forth in a comfortable rocking chair. As she did, she hummed an old, favorite tune: and her fingers flew as she went about mending one of little Anita's dresses.

She smiled when she heard a soft rapping at the door; she had expected Jason Mankiller to return even sooner.

She wished she hadn't unquestioningly flung the door so wide open when she saw standing there on its threshold not Jason, but two men who were complete strangers to her: one young, the other middle-aged.

The younger one seemed to turn tongue-tied at the sight of her, so his companion elbowed him lightly in the ribs. At that, both men doffed their hats courteously.

"Mrs. Mendoza?" the older one asked.

"Yes."

"My name's Sam Dobbins. My gawking companion here is Byron Longfellow. We're friends of Jason Mankiller."

"Oh. Won't you come in?" she invited, taking them at their word.

"Thank you, ma'am."

"Please; have a seat," the woman offered, and they accepted. Barely had they done so when Anita came running up to Longfellow with her new dog in her arms.

"Do you wanna pet my puppy?" she asked, thrusting the mongrel forward.

"Don't bother the gentleman, Anita," her mother urged.

"Oh, it's no bother, ma'am," Byron said, smiling as he finally regained his speech faculties. "I like dogs." As proof, he began to scratch the pooch under its jaw.

"Since my partner seems to be momentarily distracted," Dobbins said, "allow me to be the one to tell you the purpose of our visit, Mrs. Mendoza."

"All right, sir."

"It has to do with the matter of a cantina located here in town. Circumstances forced the owner to vacate the premises, which now stand empty.

"The company I represent purchased that building—lock, stock and barrel—no more than an hour ago.

"Our inspection of the place showed it to be structurally sound and in need of only a minimal amount of cleaning and refurbishing: a fresh coat of whitewash on the outside and it'll be good as new.

"We hope to have it ready to reopen for business in no more than a week."

"How nice for you, Senor…Dobbins, was it?" Rosario said politely. "But what does that have to do with me?"

"It's like this, Mrs. Mendoza," Longfellow now leaped into the conversation.

"If you're really friends of Jason's," she said, "as am I—you really should just call me Rosario."

"Rosario," Byron obliged, smiling. "And we are friends of his. But we're also his business partners. It was because of his suggestion and recommendation that we came to see you."

"Oh?"

"Yes, ma'am—Rosario. You see, we've come to offer you the position of manager of the cantina when we reopen its doors."

"You have to be joking," she demurred.

"No, Ma'am," Sam declared. "We ain't. Our plan is to convert it from a cantina into being just a restaurant, and Jason done told us you're just about the best cook he ever did see."

"Then hire me as a cook, senores. Not the manager."

"No, ma'am—that just won't do. Jason was plumb insistent that he wanted you to run the place for him."

"Then why isn't he here to ask me himself?"

"Ma'am?"

"Why didn't Senor Mankiller accompany you on this visit?"

She saw the two men exchange rather pained looks.

"You mean you ain't heard what happened to him yesterday evening?"

His expression and tone of voice as he said this caused Rosario's breath to catch in her throat.

CHAPTER 24

Sunlight flashing through a nearby window awakened Mankiller. The sight of it left him feeling a bit disoriented; his last memory was of later in the day than the current angle of light would indicate.

He was also lying in a bed; but he had no memory of how he got there.

Like a man nursing a staggering hangover, he winced as the door of the room he was in banged open (though it didn't do so nearly as loudly as his pounding skull led him to believe).

Through squinting eyes he saw Jane Starr come flitting into the room, using both hands to carry a tray with a plate of food and a small pot of coffee.

"You're awake: good," she said, now gracing him with a smile. "I've brought steak, eggs and fried potatoes; and the coffee's hot and black. I expect you to finish all of it."

"How long have I been here, Jane?"

"Going on fifteen hours, I think."

"For real? How did I get here?" he murmured.

"I guess when you were declared heavyweight boxing champion of the world you became too lazy to walk up stairs on your own," she jibed. "So I had a couple of the boys carry you up."

As he painfully pushed himself up into a sitting position in the bed, Mankiller noticed that various parts of his body had been bandaged while he was out. He tensed as he realized that these wrappings and the blanket he was under were the only things covering his nakedness.

"Which one of the boys got the unpleasant job of stripping me?" he asked.

Jane smiled wickedly. "What makes you think I'd entrust such a delicate job to one of them?"

"Good Lord!" he exclaimed, and the lady gambler laughed aloud at his obvious embarrassment."

"Trust me," she told him, "stripping and bathing you was no joy. You smelled like you'd been living in a buffalo wallow."

"You bathed me, too?" She'd never seen him look so downcast.

Her own face grew more serious as she placed the food tray on his lap and took a seat next to him on the edge of the bed.

"It wasn't until I undressed you and cleaned off some of the filth that I was able to see just how awfully bruised and battered you were, Jason. And I could tell most of the damage had been inflicted *before* your brawl with that nasty Copperhead Johnson.

"We brought Doc Crotty in to work on you while you were unconscious. Believe me, he earned his pay."

Jane didn't tell him that the physician had tried to shoo her out of the room while he performed his ministrations; only to be told in no uncertain terms that she would stay and help come hell or high water.

She now wore a fresh dress in part because of the bloodstains on the one she had worn the night before: stains obtained by her having to lay atop Mankiller to keep him from deliriously thrashing about while the doctor worked on him.

Dr. Crotty had removed a bullet that had been lodged in Jason's left arm and tightly bandaged his torso due to at least two broken ribs.

He also told Jane that Jason appeared to have been cut multiple times in addition to being shot and beaten.

"You didn't get away from the Comanches that day, did you?" she said, more as a statement of fact than as a question.

"Sure I did," he countered. "How else would I be *here*?"

"Don't play word games with me," she scolded gently. "They captured you, didn't they?" He looked in her eyes and knew he couldn't lie to her.

"Yeah," he grudgingly admitted. "But the other three men with me at the station weren't near as lucky as me."

"Lucky," she said numbly. "They did horrible things to you, didn't they?"

"You don't wanna know, Jane," he replied softly. "And I don't wanna say."

He didn't tell her about the three Comancheros. He blamed them for his current condition even more than he did the Indians; and he meant to make them pay for it.

"We tried to help you," she told him. "We really did. We hardly let the horses stop at all. But it was still late the next day before we reached a settlement.

"We told them what happened, and they planned to send a party back to the depot. We couldn't think of anything more we could do."

"There wasn't," he assured her. "The important thing is that we got away in the end. What became of Mrs. Porter?"

Jane sighed. "The poor thing. She was in an awful state by the time we got here. But once we got her on a fresh stage heading out of town, she seemed to be coming around a little. I think she'll be all right once she's back in the bosom of her family."

"I hope so," he said, then began to dig into the fine breakfast Jane had brought him. For several minutes, she was content merely to watch him.

"Just one thing," she said finally. "Given the condition you were in—why in God's name did you agree to fight a behemoth like Copperhead?"

"It's not like I had much choice in the matter," he muttered defensively around a mouthful of potatoes.

"And now I hear you're trying to give the brute a job. Care to explain that one to me?"

The bounty hunter popped a cut of meat into his mouth before answering. "Sometimes when a man's down," he told her, "he just needs a hand getting up off the floor. I think Dick's the kinda fella who can stand on his own two feet once he's back on 'em."

"I hope you're right."

"Me, too. If not...next time, I'll just have to shoot 'im." Jane couldn't tell if he was joking or not.

When Jason finished off the plate of food and drained the last of the coffee, Jane took the tray and set in on a nearby table. Standing with her back to him, and apropos of nothing, she spoke.

"She's very pretty."

"Who's that?" Jason replied innocently. Jane spun and stared at him rather sternly.

"Who else? Who do you think?"

"I s'pose I'm still a little foggy, Jane," he said in a stumbling fashion. "Help me out here."

"Your...the woman you rode into town with."

"Oh. You mean Rosario. Yeah...I reckon she is a right purty girl."

Jane was inwardly steaming that the laconic drifter wasn't being more forthcoming with her, but she tried not to show it.

"The little girl is hers?"

"Yep."

Jane exhaled heavily. "And her father is...?"

"Dead."

He noticed her posture seemed to relax. "That's too bad. How did the two of them come to be with you?"

"That's kind of a long story."

"May I remind you that you're not going anywhere for awhile, Mr. Mankiller? And I've got time."

Before he could utter a reply, the door of the room flew open. Rosario and little Anita came rushing in: each clearly frantic with worry.

The child scrambled up over the foot of the bed and threw herself upon Jason, who grunted with pain as she did.

"Get down, Anita!" her mother ordered. But as she moved to lift the girl away, the bounty hunter shook his head and cradled the child in his arm.

"She's all right," he said. "She's good for what ails me." Smiling, Anita snuggled into the crook of his right arm.

"We came as soon as we heard," Rosario said, dropping down on one knee beside the bed. "What can we do?"

Before he could respond, Jane coughed rather loudly. Having failed to notice the other woman until now, Rosario rose to her feet to face the lady gambler.

"Rosario," Mankiller said, "I'd like you to meet Jane Starr. Jane, this is Rosario Mendoza."

The drifter lowered his face to give Anita a kiss on top of her head, and so didn't notice the two women warily appraising each other: like two boxers upon first entering the ring.

"I'll leave you to your company," Jane said tersely, snatching up the food tray and heading for the door of the room.

"Do you have to go so soon?" Jason asked.

"Yes. I have to get ready for work."

Jason expected she would return that night, after the saloon closed. But she didn't. He didn't know why.

Nor did he know why it bothered him so much that she didn't.

CHAPTER 25

Mankiller slept only fitfully that night: mainly due to lingering physical pain. Every time he turned in his sleep, he put pressure on something that hurt.

As dawn approached, he decided to give up and get out of bed. When he pushed himself to his feet, he momentarily thought he had made a mistake, for he swayed as unsteadily as a ship pitching on the ocean.

The worst of that moment passed quickly, though, and in small steps he moved across the room. Progressing slowly, pausing once to lean on a chair for support, he made his way to the window and took a seat on the sill.

Expecting to see nothing but other buildings, he was somewhat surprised that there was already activity on the street below.

He witnessed a cluster of about half a dozen young boys gathering just outside the front of the saloon. He recognized one of them as being his "partner," the newsboy Toby. The reason for this early morning congregation soon became evident.

Moving through the doors of The Bloody Eye and out onto the walkway was one of Sam Dobbins' hired swampers. The man's job at the moment, at which he seemed to be proficient, was to sweep out the previous day's sawdust: the favored material used to cover the floors of saloons for the purpose of soaking up spilled drinks and other fluids.

Sometimes, these dustings would also contain coins or tiny nuggets of gold that patrons of the saloon had dropped the night before and had failed or not bothered to retrieve.

Once such leavings were swept out along with the sawdust, they became fair game for anyone who could lay claim to them.

"Come 'n' git it, ya guttersnipes!" the swamper yelled to the boys as he made his final swipe with his broom.

The instant the sawdust left the sidewalk and hit the dirt street, the boys who had gathered there began a mad scramble for it.

Occasionally, punching and kicking was involved.

None was more aggressive in the hunt for small treasures than was young Toby. Even as his elbows and knees flailed about, he never took his eyes off the prize.

And when the dust literally settled, Jason saw him proudly walking away with a couple of coins in his possession.

The drifter smiled sadly and shook his head.

Then, feeling suddenly tired, he limped back to his bed and was finally able to fall into a slightly deeper and more restful sleep.

This time, he awakened only because he heard a soft rapping on the door of his room.

"Come."

The door swung open slowly as Rosario Mendoza backed into the room. This time, it was she who came bearing a tray of food for the bounty hunter.

Jason could tell by its offerings—eggs scrambled with salsa, onions and peppers, tortillas stuffed with shredded chicken—that the woman had most likely prepared the meal personally. He partook of it heartily.

"I won't be able to stay and visit," she announced once she saw him well underway with his meal. "There's a lot of work to be done on the restaurant if we're going to get it reopened as soon as Senor Sam would like."

"I understand."

"Thank you for giving me this opportunity," she said.

"You already thanked me yesterday, remember?"

"I just want you to know how grateful I am, Jason."

"*Por nada.*" He took a sip of milk. "Hell, if the quality of the meals served there is up to the standard of what you've always fed me—it'll be the townsfolk who owe me a debt of gratitude."

She smiled and patted his arm.

"There is just one thing I'd like to discuss with you," he said. "Just briefly. It won't take but a minute."

"Of course."

"You know that I'm one of the owners of the cantina?"

"Yes. That's why I accepted the job."

"Good. Good. I just want you to know that I intend to keep my hands off the place; it's yours to run as you see fit. The day-to-day operations are completely under your control."

"But...?" she said, cocking her head to one side and smiling.

He chuckled lightly. "But...I would like to ask one favor of you: in regard to the hiring of help."

CHAPTER 26

After finishing his breakfast, Mankiller found he was able to sleep again, and did so.

He awakened for good sometime in the early afternoon, though, and quickly grew bored and restless just lying in bed.

He had just risen to begin a search for any type of clothing when the door to his room was flung open and Jane Starr came breezing in.

Scrambling to cover his nakedness, Jason's legs got tangled in the bed covers and he fell to the floor.

"Ohh!" Jane rushed over to him and helped him back into bed.

"Dammit, woman," he groused. "You might try knocking before you just waltz in on a man!"

He scowled when she replied with laughter. "Did you forget you no longer have anything I haven't already seen?"

The reminder rendered him even more flushed, which in turn invited more laughter from her.

Then his face grew suddenly serious, and inwardly he began to curse himself for being such a careless fool.

"What is it, Jason?" a concerned Jane asked. "Did you re-injure yourself?"

"My gunbelt," he said tersely. "Bring me my gun, Janie."

"All right."

She walked across the room and opened its single small closet. Mankiller could see it was mostly bare, save for the buckskin shirt he had worn into town. This gift from Three Pony, suspended from a wooden hanger, appeared to have been freshly washed. From a narrow shelf, Jane took down the bounty hunter's gun and holster, bringing them to him.

He draped the gunbelt over the bedpost on his left, positioning it so the pistol it held would be within quick and easy reach when he was lying down.

"Surely you're not in any danger here," Jane said.

"Prob'ly not. But you can never be too careful, darlin'. I hate to admit it, but there's plenty o' ne'er-do-wells out there who'd gladly slip in here and murder me in my sleep."

The thought of such an assassination attempt made the woman visibly shiver.

"Don't worry," he told her. "I ain't gonna let that happen. But from now on, what say we keep the door over there locked?"

"Of course."

"And scrounge me up some decent *clothes*!"

Sitting on the bed beside where he lay, Jane was again able to laugh. "I'll be glad to carry out the first request.

"But you don't need any clothes just yet. Dr. Crotty said he wants you to stay abed for at least a few days." She was unmoved by Jason's glare.

"Well, at least bring me a nightshirt or some long johns," he pled, "so's I can move around the room without lettin' Old Glory shine!"

"That I can do," she replied.

"And I'll tell you somethin', darlin'," he said. "Ain't nothin' them poor, simple savages did to me gonna kill me—but *boredom* might. Just as surely, if not as swiftly, as a bullet would."

"I've already thought of that," she countered, lifting up a small bundle she had carried into the room with her and depositing it on the night table next to the bed.

"I've brought you books," she said, and noticed his eyes light up.

"I lost the ones I had in my luggage, along with everything else, back at the stage station. The local mercantile didn't have a very large selection, but I found a few volumes I thought you might like. Including this one."

She placed into his eager hands a copy of the second Jason Mankiller dime novel she had written, eliciting a smile from the drifter.

"This is just fine," he said, then looked up at her. "Is this mine to keep?"

"Of course. They all are."

He handed the thin penny dreadful back to her. "Then I'd like it real well if you'd be kind enough to sign it for me, personal." Smiling, she took it and hugged it to her bosom.

"I'm gonna have to find another copy of your first book, too. My old dog-eared copy got left behind with my dead horse at the depot."

At that moment, again without the warning of a knock, the door swung inward.

As it did, Copperhead Johnson ambled into the room.

Mankiller shoved Jane aside with his left hand, dumping her unceremoniously onto the floor, then drew his gun with his right. As he swung it around, he saw the big man was again holding up empty hands.

"I ain't armed!" Johnson yelped.

"What the hell do you mean, just barging in here like that!" Jane scolded. It was clear, as she rose from the floor rubbing her backside that she was in no mood to be trifled with.

"I'm sorry, Miss Jane," Copperhead said contritely. "I apologize, Mr. Mankiller," he directed to the drifter; his manner much more sedate than it had been when first they'd met.

"And I'm real sorry about the other night, too. Drunk or not, if I'd known you was already all stove up on account o' the Injuns—I'd never have picked a fight with you."

"Well just don't go makin' a habit of it, Copperhead," Jason said.

"I don't aim to." The big man then chuckled and rubbed his discolored jaw. "It's probably a damn good thing that you was under the weather—else ya mighta killed me!"

"I just got lucky."

"So did I," Johnson said earnestly. "I wanna thank ya fer recommendin' me fer that park guard position.

"You got my promise I'll do the best job I can. We're gonna make that park safe enough ta hold prayer meetin's in."

"I'm gonna hold you to that promise, Dick," Jason told him sternly but not unkindly. "And to that end, I'd advise you to lay off hittin' the bottle so hard."

"I hear ya, boss."

Johnson nodded deferentially and left the room; Jane started to follow after him.

"Don't go, Jane," Jason called out. "Stay awhile."

"Why?"

The question puzzled him slightly, but he pushed past it. "You remember how we used to sit out on the sidewalk together and have long talks?"

"I remember."

"That's what I've missed the most since I left town."

Upon hearing this, the woman's features softened and her face fully assumed the lovely cast he had been accustomed to seeing.

"I've missed those, too," she admitted.

At that moment, a girl who called herself Mona Lee, one of the soiled doves who plied her lascivious trade in the saloon below, was on her way up the stairs.

The mission she had set for herself was to entice the violently mysterious Mr. Mankiller into partaking of her carnal charms. She'd heard so many intriguing stories about the bounty hunter that she felt challenged, almost duty bound, to insinuate herself between his blankets.

As she reached the top of the stairs, she spotted Jane Starr standing in the open doorway of the room she knew belonged to Mankiller; so she paused. A moment later, Jane stepped back into the room and closed the door behind her.

Even from several feet away, Miss Mona could hear the unmistakable sound of the bolt being thrown to lock the door.

The cat-tail smiled, shrugged philosophically and headed back down the stairs.

She had no doubt the rest of her evening would prove to be more successful than had this aborted endeavor.

Certainly more lucrative.

CHAPTER 27

Within a few days, Jason and Jane were back in their old familiar spot: seated on the sidewalk to either side of the front door of The Bloody Eye.

As had become her habit, Jane always sat with a small notepad in her lap; occasionally scribbling down thoughts, ideas and observations even as she and the drifter carried on what was oft-times a lively conversation.

Jason knew that everything he told her about himself and his life might very well make it into one of her stories: probably in a remarkably embellished form. Still, he was almost totally open with her: much more so than with any other person he had ever known. He also had complete trust that nothing she wrote would ever be deliberately intended to cast him in a bad light.

Mankiller was feeling much more like his old self. He was healing nicely and was now dressed in newly purchased but familiar and comfortable clothing: black boots and trousers, a gray shirt and a black, flat-brimmed hat.

Jane noticed that even while he was carrying on a conversation with her Jason's eyes were constantly roaming over the various people who came within his field of vision. His gaze shifted from side to side often, as if he was continually assessing the situation.

She knew that, in part, this was exactly what he was doing; making sure he always knew what was going on around him. But she had come to realize that he also simply enjoyed watching people as they went about their everyday lives.

She also observed that he was playing what would seem to be a simple little game with a poker chip, wherein he continually rolled it end over end, back and forth over the top of his left hand: using his fingers to manipulate it.

Jane also knew this was no idle game or nervous habit—but rather a deliberate exercise in coordination, should the time ever come when he would need to use that hand rather than his dominant right one.

"I just noticed something," she said to him. "You're not wearing those big, fancy Spanish spurs you used to favor."

"No," he confirmed. "And I did so love them Hell rousers. But really, spurs is like chaps: not much point in wearing 'em if you ain't working cattle.

"Plus, in my newest profession," he said, lifting a booted foot and gazing at it, "I learned real quick that you'd best be able to walk quietly at all times; so as not to let folks know you're coming."

"I think I'd be afraid every minute of the day," she told him, "if I was in that profession."

"No you wouldn't."

Jane...occasionally scribbling down thoughts...

She closed her notebook and laid her pencil down.

"I haven't been sleeping well."

"Talk to me about it," he encouraged.

She did so, though she turned her face slightly away from him.

"Sometimes, I have a hard time even falling asleep. My mind just starts racing on its own and replays images from that God-awful day at the stage station.

"Then, when I do drift off, my sleep is disturbed and disrupted by dreams of it.

"They've been joined by new dreams since you came back," she told him, now returning her eyes to him.

"Just as disturbing. The images my brain conjures up about what you suffered at the hands of the Comanches are terrible to behold."

"I'm sorry," he said. "If you think it would help, I'll tell you what really happened. You might find the actual truth to be less horrifying than your imaginings."

"Yes," she said. "No...no. Don't ever tell me."

"It's your call, darlin'."

"Thank you. Hearing what really happened to you might make me feel even more guilty about leaving you behind to cover my own escape."

"You got nothin' to feel guilty about, Jane. Not one damn thing."

"Are you sure?"

"Sure as I am that the sky's blue. I chose to inject myself into that set-too before I even knew you were there. So you need to get over any such feelings you might have nagging atcha."

"I'll try."

"Cash'd prob'ly try to help you any way he could, if you'd ask him."

"I think he's fighting off some ghosts of his own, Jason. But he never talks about our brush with death that day, so neither do I.

"I am worried, though, that he might be using increased alcohol consumption to keep his nightmares at bay."

"All the more reason to try to talk to 'im, darlin'. But if he's not receptive...I'm always willing to listen to you."

"I know."

"You also need to remember that these kinds of lingering troubles are a perfectly natural response to having your life threatened.

"Hell, I'd been serving during the recent unpleasantness for nigh on to three months afore I was able to sleep all the way through the night.

"Like all wounds that don't kill you," he said, "these'll get better with time."

He knew otherwise. Such was not always the case with injuries to the heart or mind. Even now, nearly a decade gone from the war, the West was crawling with men still fighting demons that lingered from it.

Far too often, the demons won.

"And how do you sleep?" Jane asked him.

"Mostly, I sleep just fine," he told her, then smiled wistfully.

"Mostly."

"Actually," he pushed on, "one of my biggest regrets about that little dust-off at the depot is that my watch was took and I wasn't able to recover it."

"Was it valuable?"

"Oh, only to me. My daddy gave it to me. It was the last thing I had to remember him by."

"I'm sorry," she said. "But that's not entirely true, Jason. From the wonderful stories you've told me, you still own a lot of precious memories of both him and your mother."

"I do that."

"And that's more than a lot of people can say." He knew she was speaking of herself.

"Let's talk about something brighter, happier," she said after a moment of strained silence. "You know the Grand Comique is having its opening night tomorrow evening."

"I do. Sam extended a personal invite to me, to attend the gala event. I expect I'll see you and Cash there."

"Cash won't be attending, I'm afraid."

"Why not?"

"Business before pleasure," Jane told him. "Five or six high-stakes poker players have arrived in town from Dallas and Austin; and they've invited Cash to sit in with them in a private game.

"As I'm sure you know, such competitions can go on non-stop for days. We may not see him for a week."

"That being the case, Miz Starr," Jason said, leaning toward the lady gambler, "would you do me the great honor of allowing *me* to escort you to the theater?"

"I would be delighted to share your company, Mr. Mankiller," she replied airily, affecting the accent of a Southern belle and fanning her face with one hand.

"Well, then," he said, "I'll be sure to wear my best bib 'n' tucker—so's you won't be ashamed to be seen with me."

She laughed lightly: a sound Jason thought could only be matched by the sparkling rush of a mountain spring on an early spring day.

"You seem to be in fine fettle today," an approaching figure commented. Mankiller smiled and nodded in acknowledgment as Doctor Crotty stepped up onto the sidewalk.

The physician was probably a few years older than Jason, but had a boyish face that, even sporting a thin moustache, made him look younger.

"You did a fine job of patching me up, Doc," Jason complimented him.

"That's getting to be kind of a habit with you, sir," Crotty said. The bounty hunter had availed himself of the physician's services when last he was in Fort Rogers also.

"Well, it's not a very good endorsement of a doctor's skills if his patients tend *not* to make return visits, now is it?"

"Point well taken. But seriously: are you having any problems?"

"None worth mentionin'."

"So, yes. Still some lingering pain?"

"Oh, an ache here or there. Prob'ly not as bad as what a man with rheumatiz feels. Hardly noticeable."

"I'd write you a script for something if we had an apothecary here in town," the physician said. "But since we don't, just drop by my office if you feel you need a little something to take the edge off. Should I be out, my wife can fill a prescription as well as I can."

"I don't think that'll be necessary, Doc; but I'll keep it in mind."

"Have a nice day, then," Crotty said, tipping his hat to Jane before resuming his rounds.

"He seems like a nice man," she observed.

"Knows his way around a needle and thread, too," Jason added. "Patched me up nearly as good as new."

"Which is saying a lot," she commented wryly. "With the amount of thread it took, a tailor could have stitched you a new suit.'"

Mankiller chuckled, then leaned forward in his chair as he spied another familiar face passing in the street. It was the newsboy Toby, scurrying along with a bundle of freshly printed newspapers under one arm.

"Hey, Toby," Jason called.

To his mild consternation, the boy ignored him: seemingly pretending not to have heard him.

"Toby!" the drifter called more loudly. "I know you can hear me, boy. Come here."

Head hung low, the boy grudgingly approached.

"Son," Jason said gently, "did you forget our deal? You're s'posed to make sure I get a copy of each week's edition of the *Diligence* in a timely fashion."

"I know," the boy mumbled. "But I don't think ya want this one, Mr. Mankiller."

"Why's that?"

"It's not very good. There's hardly anything in it that weren't in last week's edition. It'd be a waste o' yer money."

"I'd still like to read it," Jason persisted. "C'mon—hand it over."

"All right," Toby said glumly, holding out a copy of the paper. "But just you remember: I don't write the darn thing—I just sell it."

"I know that, boy. Just give it here."

Perplexed but wanting to show the lad he held no animosity toward him, Mankiller paid for the paper Toby handed him with a dime, telling him to keep the change as usual.

The newsboy gave him a weak smile and a quick thanks, then took off running at a high gallop.

"What was that all about?" Jane asked.

"Hell if I know."

But the bounty hunter realized immediately what had the boy upset when he opened the paper to see a front-page editorial entitled "A Killer in Our Midst."

The opinion piece had been written by the newspaper's publisher/editor, Ezra Vail.

Mankiller read the editorial from start to finish, chuckling several times as he did. He then handed the paper to Jane, who read the piece aloud.

A notorious gunman is once more walking the streets of Fort Rogers, with complete impunity. Failure to take action against him is a disgrace to all that is lawful and decent.

Such a two-legged animal as Jackson [sic] Mankiller should not and cannot be accepted into the company of good, God-fearing folk: any more than would be a rabid dog or skunk.

Speaking plainly, this sorry excuse for a human being seems to revel in living up to his violent surname. He is a heartless, cold-blooded killer, said to have shed the blood of scores of men.

Less than 24 hours after returning to our fair city, this relentless bounty hunter virtually beat an innocent man to death with his bare hands.

It is also a well-known fact that this creature shuns the company of the upright; instead preferring to consort with the foulest elements of society.

*   The conclusion to be drawn from this is inescapable. If Fort Rogers ever hopes to be thought of as a truly civilized metropolis— it should run the likes of Jackson Mankiller out of town!*

"Sounds to me like Mr. Vail has you pegged pretty well," Jane said calmly, handing the paper back to Jason.

"Don't it, though?" he replied, stretching his legs out leisurely. "Of course, you know, darlin'—that makes *you* part of that 'foul element' I consort with."

"I've been called worse."

"I'm not surprised."

"So," she said, smiling, "what sort of gown do you think I should wear to the theater tomorrow night?"

Mankiller laughed.

CHAPTER 28

Ezra Vail sat slumped over his desk, laboriously working on an obituary he was writing for one of the local barbers who had just passed away. The proper wording of death notices was trickier than the average person might realize.

He exhaled in mild exasperation as one of his printers tapped on the frame of his doorless office.

"What is it?" he asked.

"There's a gentleman out front, says he'd like to speak with you, Mr. Vail."

"Did he give you his name?"

"Didn't have to," the printer gulped. "It's that Mankiller fella."

Involuntarily, Vail stiffened and his heart rate quickened as he stiffly pushed himself to his feet.

"Want me to slip out the back and go fetch the law?" the printer asked.

"I don't think there'll be any need for that," Vail said, then added in a softer voice, "and if there is—it's probably already too late."

Stepping around his dumbfounded employee, Vail stepped out into the main part of the shop. He saw instantly that the man waiting patiently on the opposite side of the front counter was indeed the infamous bounty hunter. There was no mistaking that distinctive face.

"You Mr. Vail?" the drifter asked as the publisher drew closer.

"I am," Vail replied, cringing as he heard his voice crack slightly.

"I got some business I'd like to discuss with you," Jason said, holding up a rolled copy of the latest edition of the *Diligence* and using it to point at Vail. His stony face completely hid whatever emotion he was feeling at the moment.

"What sort of business?" Vail managed to squeeze out. He was frankly amazed at the response he received.

"First off, Mr. Vail, let me compliment you on the overall quality of your little paper."

"Huh?"

"Yessir. I've always found it to be highly informative. And usually purty well written, too."

"Thank you?"

With slow deliberation, Jason slid a piece of paper from his shirt pocket, unfolding it before spreading it out on the counter top.

Vail's eyes widened slightly when he looked down and saw it to be a simple, hand-drawn mock-up of an advertising flyer: announcing that *Rosario's Restaurant* was now open for business and offering quality food for breakfast, lunch and supper.

"Here's my question," Jason said. "How much would it cost me to have this here flyer done up professional-like, then run it as a full-page ad in ever' edition of the *Diligence* for the next month?

"Plus, printed up as a poster—say, 25 copies—and posted and displayed all over the part of town west of the Deadline? Bottom line it for me, sir."

"Are you serious?" Vail gasped.

"As a bullet in the belly."

Convinced of the drifter's sincerity, Vail pulled out from under the counter a small notepad and the stub of a pencil and set doing work doing the figures.

"I can do the job for you," he said tentatively, "for four dollars?"

"Is that an answer, or a question?" Jason replied.

Vail cleared his throat. "An answer."

"Sounds fair to me," Mankiller said, pulling a folded wad of bills out of a pants pocket and counting out the required amount.

"There's a little fella works for you, delivering papers," he then said without looking up at Vail. "Name o' Toby."

"Ah, yes. A good boy."

"I think so. He's a hard worker, and I can tell he's bright."

"You're right. Especially for being mostly self-taught the way he is."

"How's that?"

"Well, his mama's done the best she can by Toby and the girls. But between working and looking for work and having to raise the young ones alone, she hasn't been able to teach them more than the basics.

"I have noticed that, since about the last time you were in town, Toby's taken to reading every edition I put out, from front to back. It usually takes him a few days to do it, and he has to ask me or one of my assistants to explain some words and stories to him: but he always sticks with it until he's read every article."

"It's good that you take the time to help him."

"It's no bother. I think he'd go far if he could get some formal schooling."

"Any reason why he can't?"

"Just the fact that Fort Rogers doesn't actually have a school yet."

"Folks need to do something about that."

"They will, some day. And when they do, Toby's just one of the children who'll benefit from it."

The bounty hunter now raised his face to the editor, who winced slightly at the sight.

"It's my wish that he always be treated fairly."

"I assure you he always has been. Always will be."

"Good." Jason then headed for the exit, but stopped and turned back as he opened the door.

"Oh," he said, again pointing the rolled-up newspaper in his hand at Vail like an accusing finger, "there is one more thing."

"Yes?" Vail said hoarsely, recoiling slightly from the out-thrust paper.

"In your editorial this week…you got my first name wrong. It's 'Jason'—not 'Jackson'."

"I'll remember that, Mr. Mankiller," Vail said, exhaling deeply and stiffening his spine, "the next time I write such a piece."

"I'd appreciate it," Jason replied, raising the rolled paper to the brim of his hat as if in a salute before exiting the building.

Blinking as beads of rolling perspiration stung his eyes, Vail picked up the hand-drawn advertisement from the counter top—and noticed to his chagrin that the hand holding it was trembling slightly.

Just outside the door of the newspaper office, Jason smiled wickedly. Then he noticed a woman standing in the street near the sidewalk in front of him; gazing at him.

She was a not-unattractive woman with light brown hair: but a rather worn look on her face made her appear older than she probably was. The bounty hunter stepped off the sidewalk and approached her.

"Mr. Mankiller?" Her voice was hesitant, but sounded more tired than harried or afraid.

"Yes?"

"I'm Sarah Applegate."

Only now did Jason notice the young newsboy Toby; peeking out at him from behind the skirts of the woman he now assumed to be the boy's mother.

"Did you kill Mr. Vail?" Toby inquired.

"Toby!" his mother snapped.

"Not today, I didn't," Jason responded in mock seriousness. He shifted his gaze to the mother and gallantly doffed his hat.

"What can I do for you, ma'am?"

"I think you've already done it," she replied, a warm smile now creasing her face and erasing years from it. "I started my new waitressing job at Rosario's yesterday. Pays a real decent wage, too."

"I'm glad to hear that," Jason said. "But I think you're giving me too much credit and thanking the wrong person. Miz Mendoza does all the hiring and firing for her place—not me."

"I'm not trying to embarrass you," Sarah assured him. "But Rosario already told me it was your idea to hire me."

"And I'm sure you'll do a real good job," the drifter told her. "Ain't that right, Toby?"

"She sure will!" the boy said emphatically, stepping out from behind his mother.

"Was the size of my salary your idea, too?" the woman persisted.

"I think you'll find Rosario needs no prompting from me to treat people fair," he said, being truthful while nimbly dodging the question. No need to shame this good woman by telling her his wish was that young Toby would no longer have to fight in the dirt for pennies.

"Still, if you don't mind me asking," the woman persisted. "We've never even met that I know of, before today. Why have you taken such an interest in me and my family?"

Mankiller detected no hint of suspicion in her question: just pure and understandable curiosity.

"Well, ma'am," he told her, "it's like this." He nodded toward Toby. "In case he hasn't told you, Mr. Applegate there and me are business associates." The boy drew himself up more erect.

"He looks out for me—and I do the same for him and his. It's that simple. Now, if you'll excuse me." He donned his hat, feeling an uncomfortable need to beat a retreat.

"Just one more thing," the woman said, moving closer and cutting off his escape. "At least allow me to repay your kindness: say, with supper with the children and me?"

"There's no need for you to do that," Jason replied, patting his hard, flat stomach. "I've already ate so much since I got back inta town that I'm starting to develop quite a table muscle."

"It would be my pleasure," she insisted. He could tell from the hardscrabble woman's demeanor that this gesture was important to her as a matter of pride.

"I s'pect it'll be *my* pleasure," the told her. "I'd be honored to break bread with you."

"Does fried chicken suit your taste? Maybe some blackberry cobbler?"

"I wouldn't say no to either, Miz Applegate."

"Shall we make it Sunday, then? About six o'clock?"

"Six o'clock it is. I'll look forward to it."

"As will I, Mr. Mankiller," she said cheerfully. Rising up on her toes, she lightly gave him a peck on the cheek; then quickly turned and hurried off.

Toby followed along after her, looking back over his shoulder at the drifter and grinning.

Mankiller brushed the cheek Sarah Applegate had kissed with the back of two fingers, awkwardly shuffled his feet in the dust a bit, then set out in the direction of The Bloody Eye saloon.

The new name of the place still made him cringe.

CHAPTER 29

Mankiller sat alone in his room, reading by the light coming in through its sole window.

He softly chuckled aloud, not for the first time. He was well into the latest dime novel Jane Starr had written about his supposedly "true" adventures, and having a delightful time of it.

The mostly fictional version of him she had created seemed to have been cobbled together from equal parts of Wild Bill Hickok, Jesse James and Robin Hood. Along with, he noted appreciatively, just a dash of Sir Lancelot.

It was long on far-fetched action (Just how many times did Eastern readers think a man could fire a revolver without needing to reload?) and melodramatic emotive scenes (doubtless intended to tug at the heartstrings of any female readers): but was not without a certain elegant flair in its style and use of language.

As he had told her repeatedly, his Janie girl clearly had talent. So good was she, in fact, that he often found himself worrying for the hero's continued survival.

For all its exaggerations and mythic overtones, there were passages wherein the book also came almost uncomfortably close to painting a true and accurate portrait of him. Those moments he found to be somewhat less enjoyable and entertaining.

When a woman gets to know a man that well, begins to burrow that deeply beneath his skin to what lies below, it can be more frightening than is staring down the barrel of a loaded gun.

He scowled slightly when a strong knock came at his door: he was in the middle of a particularly thrilling chapter and hated having to put the book down.

As he crossed the room, his right hand reflexively went to the butt of his pistol in its cross-draw holster. He went to one side so as not to be standing directly in front of the door, thus placing himself out of any possible line of fire should the caller waiting on the other side of the portal have ill intent.

"Who is it?"

"Marshal Russell."

Recognizing the voice, Mankiller relaxed his stance and opened the door. The top city lawman nodded in silent greeting as he entered the room. The bounty hunter tensed slightly as a second man pushed in behind Russell: a man he did not know. He remained prepared for trouble even after he spotted the star pinned to this man's vest.

"Mankiller," Russell said, "this is Sheriff Aaron Stimson, from the county seat."

"Sheriff," Jason said. He motioned to a pair of chairs at the nearby table. "Take a seat, gents.

"State your business," he said stiffly as the two lawmen seated themselves.

"Don't get on yer high horse with me, youngster," Sheriff Stimson shot back. He was a tall and stocky man of probably forty years. His dark and weathered face spoke of long time spent in the sun. "I'm here ta do you a favor."

"What kind of favor?"

"Well, more of a warning, really."

Jason's hackles rose. "What is it you think I've done?"

"Not that kind o' warning. I got no beef with you."

"Good. Speak your peace."

Stimson stared down at the floor a few seconds before beginning. "Much as I hate to admit it, we had a prisoner bust out o' the county jail a couple nights ago."

"Kinda careless of ya, wasn't it?"

The sheriff glared at him. "He had help."

"You don't think it was me that sprung him, do ya?"

"No. 'Course not."

"Then why should this concern me?"

"The man who escaped was Nathan McClure."

If the peace officer expected this revelation to spark a response from the bounty hunter, he was sorely disappointed.

"Never heard of 'im."

"Are you joking?" Stimson asked, but could see by Jason's expression that he wasn't.

"Why, hell, boy...all you done was kill damn near every one of his kinfolk earlier this year."

"Oh."

Now the name struck home. When Mankiller first came to Fort Rogers, he had been provoked into a gunfight by a worthless cur named Zeb McClure.

The results were fatal—for McClure.

Unwilling to leave it go at that, several other members of the McClure clan and some of their hired guns had become hell-bent on returning the favor by burying Jason.

Instead, they'd served as the catalyst for his decision to become a bounty hunter—when he collected the rewards on all their heads.

"You say he had help bustin' outta jail?"

"I did. It was his shiftless kid brother, Lem. The two of 'em damn near killed a deputy o' mine. As it is, he prob'ly won't ever walk right."

"And now comes the warning," Jason said, smiling slightly. "You think they mean to come after me?"

"I know they do," Stimson said grimly. "'Fore he passed out from the pain o' the pistol whippin' and stompin' they did on 'im, my deputy heard Lem tell Nathan you'd shown up here in Fort Rogers. Since both of 'em was known to have publicly threatened ta kill you first chance they got, it ain't hard ta figger out where they're gonna show up.

"That's why I come ta warn ya. Now, don't get me wrong, bounty man: I don't give a rat's ass if they blow yer brains out. But McClure escaped from my jail: him and his brother worked my deputy over somethin' awful in the process.

"Whether you do it, I do it, or Marshal Russell does it, I don't care. But I want 'em stopped. Savvy?"

"Yeah, I savvy," Jason replied. "You're hangin' me out as bait to draw the two of 'em into your sights."

"You can look at it that way, boy," Stimson said, his lips curling slightly. "Or you can think of it as an opportunity.

"There's a sizeable reward on both of 'em. Capture 'em—or kill 'em—before they can kill you…and you can collect it."

"I'll do that," Jason said as the two peace officers rose to leave.

"I'll be in town a couple days," Stimson told him, "takin' care o' some court business. And who knows: if one of us badge packers spots 'em first, you may have nothin' ta worry about."

"I ain't worried now," Mankiller told him.

Stimson had a comeback on the tip of his tongue, but refrained from using it when he saw the ominous expression on the drifter's face. So instead, he merely nodded curtly and headed for the door.

Marshal Russell lingered a moment, extracting some papers from his shirt pocket and handing them to Jason.

"Dodgers with pictures of the two of 'em," he explained. "So's you'll know 'em if you see 'em."

"Thanks, Marshal," Jason said sincerely. "I appreciate it."

"Mebbe they won't even come here," Russell said. "If they're smart, they've done took off for the tall uncut."

"They don't look to be that smart," Jason commented, unfolding the posters and examining the faces there upon.

The Marshal nodded somberly before following the sheriff out the door and leaving Mankiller once again alone.

He studied the posters for a few minutes, fixing the details of the outlaws' faces in his mind. Then he tossed the flyers aside and returned to his seat by the window.

The pages of his book still waited.

CHAPTER 30

All in attendance would later agree that the opening night at the Grand Comique Theater was a rousing success.

The inside of the imposing new structure itself had been decorated in what was indeed a grand style. The three hallways leading from the front lobby to the seating sections of the main auditorium contained their own special form of entertainment: one that scandalized some but titillated, amused and enchanted most.

Large, recessed niches set into the walls of these corridors were used to display *tableaux vivant*.

These could best be described as living dioramas, wherein live models—all of them women and all scantily clad—posed in recreations of famous scenes from art and history. The one portraying a nearly naked Eve accepting the forbidden fruit from the serpent seemed to be an especial favorite of viewers.

Mankiller recognized a few of the models in these tableaux to be soiled doves recruited from the local talent pool.

As promised, the headliner and Master of Ceremonies on stage for opening night had been the renowned Eddie Foy: comedian and song-and-dance man extraordinaire. Featured acts included singers, dancers, jugglers, magicians and even a lady contortionist.

When singer Lottie Rogers—"the Leadville Nightingale"—performed her heartfelt rendition of "You Never Miss Your Sainted Mother Till She's Dead and Gone to Heaven," there remained scarcely a dry eye in the house.

The songstress graciously allowed the approving audience to coax her back on the stage for two encores.

In the next edition of the *Diligence*, Ezra Vail would be effusive in his praise of both the theater and the performers it presented.

"That was marvelous!" Jane Starr enthused as she and Mankiller joined the crowd filing out of the facility.

"I'm glad you enjoyed it," Jason said.

"Didn't you?"

"Sure I did."

"Truly?"

"Darlin'," he assured her, slipping his arm through hers and taking her hand, "I had a hog-killin' time!"

As a cap to the evening, he escorted Jane to the Hansen House to partake of a late supper. They were immediately ushered to a reserved table, which Jane silently noted was positioned in a back corner in such a way as to facilitate Jason's habit of never sitting with his back to a room.

Jane dined on grilled prairie chicken smothered in a sauce of creamed green onions, while Jason indulged in a thick bear steak. Both ate ears of roasted corn and pickled tomatoes. While Jane sipped a fine wine, Jason allowed himself the luxury of a cold beer.

A single candle cast a warm, pale glow over their table. A solo violinist strolled through the dining room, playing softly for the pleasure of all.

"I'm not sure which drew more stares at the Comique," Jane commented at one point, "the naked women in the tableaux—or *you*."

"Sex and violence, darlin'," he waxed philosophically, "Neither ever fails to draw attention to itself."

"After seeing you get more of that attention than he and his wife did," she observed, "I think the mayor would have happily engaged in either!"-0

"Must not be an election year," Jason shot back, "or he would have."

"Not that he isn't already campaigning for another term," Jane huffed. "He's taking all the credit for the financial growth in town."

"Ah. And who does he blame for what goes on in the Tenderloin?"

"The Republicans, of course."

"Of course."

He smiled at her after taking a sip of his beer. "Y'know, I noticed you got more than your share of admiring glances yourself this evening, little lady."

"Oh, go on."

"It's true. From men and women both."

"Don't be silly."

"Hand on the Bible. And no wonder. Compared to every other woman who was in that theater tonight—in the audience or on the stage—you're a huckleberry above a persimmon."

"You have quite a streak of gallantry in you, sir."

"I got eyes; that's all it takes."

"Thank you," she said warmly, "for showing me such a good time."

"Believe me, darlin', it's been equally pleasurable for me."

"It has been a wonderful evening, hasn't it, Jason?" she asked, laying a hand on his arm.

"One of the best I've ever had," he assured her. "The kind you wish would never end."

As the couple was nearing the conclusion of their meal, they heard a bit

A single candle cast a warm, pale glow...

of a muted uproar coming from the vicinity of the hotel lobby.

"Look," exclaimed a man seated at a nearby table, "it's that feller from the Comique (which he mispronounced as 'commie-cue')!"

At that, Jane and Jason saw both Eddie Foy and Lottie Rogers enter the dining room, escorted by a beaming Sam Dobbins.

Spying his two friends at the back of the room, Sam softly spoke to Foy, who brightened and nodded enthusiastically.

Sighing softly and wiping his mouth with a napkin, Mankiller rose to his feet as Sam led the two entertainers toward his table.

"Mr. Foy, Miss Rogers—allow me to introduce my good friend, Jason Mankiller! Jason, I'm sure you recognize my guests."

The drifter managed a smile as he extended his right hand. Foy happily pumped it several times; Lottie's handshake was gentler and lingered.

"Please meet my lovely dinner companion," Jason said, indicating Jane. "Miz Jane Starr."

Both gave her a perfunctory nod and smile, but it was clear that the bounty hunter commanded their full attention.

"My compliments on your performances this evening," he told them. "It's indeed an honor to have two such famous people grace Fort Rogers with their presence."

"And it's an honor to meet someone equally famous," Foy said magnanimously. "Your exploits have caused quite a stir back East, Mr. Mankiller."

"Well, I reckon better than most, Mr. Foy, you know you should only believe half of what you hear—and none of what you read."

Still, it was evident that Foy was somewhat in awe of the bounty hunter. To Jane's eye, it seemed that the Leadville Nightingale was deriving even more pleasure than the comedian was from being in Jason's proximity.

"Jane and I have already finished our supper," Mankiller told them, "but we were just about to enjoy some coffee and a little dessert. Would you care to join us?"

Almost simultaneously, Foy said, "Oh, we wouldn't want to intrude—" while Lottie gushed, "We'd love to!"

Jane raised her wine glass to her lips to hide the smile on her face as Lottie quickly moved to plant herself in the empty chair closest to the bounty hunter, sliding it even nearer and letting her hand rest on his forearm and give it a little squeeze. Jane leaned close to Jason from the other side and whispered in his ear.

"Careful, darling...or you might end up *being* dessert!"

CHAPTER 31

Marshal Clayton Russell was at his desk filling out requisition forms when a knock came at the front door of the jail and Jason Mankiller entered.

"Can you spare a few minutes, Marshal?"

"I suppose," the lawman replied, motioning the drifter in. "Have a seat. Care for a cup of coffee?"

"I'll take both, thanks."

"I've been meaning to talk to you anyway," Russell said as he handed Jason a tin cup filled nearly to the brim.

"Have the McClure boys been spotted in town?"

"No. Nary a sign of 'em. Sheriff Stimson's beginning to think they mighta rethought their plan and headed for the border instead."

"That would be fine with me."

"Me, too. Stimson's just about finished with his work here, and then he'll be heading home." Russell paused, rubbing his rough hands together. "It was somethin' else I wanted to talk to you about."

"No trouble, I hope."

"No, no. Not at all. I just wanted to tell you that I followed your advice and had a serious talk with the Mayor and the City Council."

0"How'd that go?"

"Real well. I can't say they were happy about the subject matter, but they mostly agreed with my request for a piece o' the pie and a little more job security."

"I figgered they would."

"And they seemed downright relieved when I allowed 'em to talk me down to keeping only twenty percent of the amount of fees and fines I collect."

"They'll still be getting their money's worth," Jason opined, blowing gently on his coffee before taking a drink.

"I got the feeling they knew the day would come when I'd make such demands, and were prepared for that eventuality.

"And I'm real sure that dropping your name into the mix like you suggested sealed the deal." Russell stared down at his own cup, unsure of how to say what followed.

"I want to thank you for your help."

"Think nothin' of it, Marshal. I've been close enough to the workings of the law to be convinced that the occupational hazards faced by any decent peace officer are worth a whole helluva lot more than the salary most of 'em draw.

"When a man risks death, he oughtta be paid accordingly. It's that simple."

"Well, it's appreciated. Now, what can I do for you?"

"I could use a little assistance myself," Mankiller told him.

He then briefly recounted for the marshal the story of the battle with the Comanches at the relay station. Unknown to him, Russell had already heard multiple tellings of the tale, having questioned the other three survivors upon their arrival in Fort Rogers.

He made no mention of the fact that Mankiller's heroic deeds played a much larger role in their versions than they did in his own telling.

Jason didn't bother to make more than a passing mention of his brief captivity and torture, choosing to end his narrative by telling of the three Comancheros who had aided the Indians: and of his intent to now hunt them down.

"I don't know that I can be of help in identifying any of them," Russell admitted. "The usual stomping ground for that bunch is west of here and well out of my jurisdiction."

"I figgered as much. But I also thought it possible that one or more of 'em mighta made their way onto a dodger that's made its way across your desk."

He proceeded to describe the three outlaws. The details of the three men's appearances had been branded into his brain; and were as clear and sharp now as the day he first confronted them.

"Now that I think on it," Russell said when Jason finished, "and having those descriptions—I just might be able to help you after all."

The marshal rose and walked over to his file cabinet; began thumbing through the sheaf of wanted posters that had accumulated since the last time the bounty hunter was in town.

Finding the dodger he sought, the lawman pulled it out of the files and laid it on his desk in front of Mankiller. The bounty hunter found himself looking down at an illustration of a man who definitely looked like the one-eyed Anglo who had so gladly handed him over to the Comanches. The written description beneath the drawing even made mention of the outlaw's missing finger.

The man depicted on the poster was identified as being Rueben Keeler. He carried with him a $500 bounty—dead or alive—for armed robbery and murder.

"I've never laid eyes on this man in person," Marshal Russell said, "only the picture on the dodger. And the half-breed you mentioned doesn't sound familiar at all.

"But I may know who their Mexican compadre is."

"Anything you can tell me would be appreciated."

"I'm not sayin' it's him for certain sure, mind you. But there was a Mex cibolero who used to show up here in town from time to time: always hauling a wagonload of buffalo hides.

"The fella's name, as best I can recall, was Rodrigo Chavez.

"I only had a few run-ins with him; other than one drunk and disorderly, he always managed to stay clear of jail here in Fort Rogers.

"I also recall being told by Chavez on that occasion that the place he hangs his hat most of the time is a little village called Rio Caballo."

Mankiller repeated the name of the man and the village, burning both into his brain.

"Much obliged, Marshal." He tapped the poster on the desk. "Mind if I keep this flyer on Keeler?"

"Nope." The lawman motioned toward his file cabinet. "Feel free to take any of 'em you want."

"I'll do that," Jason replied, rolling up the dodger on Keeler.

"I assume this means you'll be leaving town again soon," Russell said.

"Soon."

"Then you must be slipping, bounty man. You ain't killed a single person during this stay."

"It wasn't for lack o' tryin', Marshal," Jason retorted, thinking of his bloody brawl with Copperhead Dick Johnson.

"Seriously, though," the lawman warned him, "you'd best be sure you're fully healed and rested before you set out after the likes of Keeler and Chavez. Comancheros have a rep for being a bad lot—and they've earned it.

"I know firsthand that Chavez has. On one of his layovers here, a breed made the mistake of challenging him to a knife fight.

"By the time Chavez got through cutting up the breed—the man's own mother wouldn't have been able to recognize him."

"How'd Chavez escape doing jail time for that?"

Russell shrugged. "The witnesses all agreed that Chavez had been the challenged party, so I had no call to arrest him."

As if fearing that Mankiller thought he had been too scared to take on the Mexican, and not sure he would have been wrong to do so, Russell added, "But I strongly suggested to Chavez that he get outta town. That was the last we ever saw of him." The lawman pointed a finger at Jason.

"If his friends are as mean as he is—you'd best be real careful."

"Thanks for the warning, Marshal," Mankiller said, heading for the door.

"But it's the three o' them that need to be afraid."

CHAPTER 32

After having enjoyed yet another fine supper at the Hansen House, Mankiller invited Jane Starr to join him for a leisurely stroll through the town's new park.

He had initially suggested dining at Rosario Mendoza's restaurant, but for some reason Jane had felt disinclined to do so. She seemed more than happy to dine with him elsewhere, though, and to accept his invitation to a walk.

"I have to say," she commented after a few minutes, "that Sam and Byron and whoever did the actual design for this park did a wonderful job."

"I couldn't agree more," Jason said.

The wide, grassy areas of the park were lush and well tended. Gravel-covered pathways wound their way back and forth throughout. Benches were conveniently placed about; more than one occupied by young couples obviously in the early, dizzying days of courtship. Others, like he and Jane, simply walked the expanse, enjoying the fresh air and the cool of the evening. Some had brought blankets to sit upon after laying them on the ground. A few were picnicking.

Existing trees had been maintained and new saplings added; the landscape was dotted with multiple beds of flowers. Lampposts conveniently spaced kept the entirety of the walking paths well lit.

In the center of the park a large hole was being excavated that, in time, would be filled with water to form a man-made pond.

At Jane's suggestion, Sam Dobbins had agreed to stock it with a few fish and to bring in ducks that patrons of the park (especially children) would be encouraged to feed with bread crumbs.

"I've always been pretty much a city girl," Jane told him. "But there really is something almost magical about being out in nature. You can almost imagine Adam and Eve walking through a scene like this."

"You don't have to imagine it," Jason said with a smile. "Just go look at the gal in the tableau over to the Comique."

Jane swatted his arm lightly.

"But I know what you mean," he said. "Now, try to imagine what it's like in the true wild, high up in the Rockies."

"You used to trap there with your father before he died, didn't you?"

"You remember that?"

She smiled, put an arm through his and pressed closer. "You're not the only one who listens, you know?" He chuckled softly.

"What was it like there?" she asked.

"Untamed. Unspoiled. Free." The woman smiled as she looked up at his face and saw a faraway look in his eyes.

"I s'pect me and pa saw places no other white man had ever seen before. Mebbe no red man, either.

"Alone out there, you become a part of it. As much as the trees and the rocks and the rivers and the animals are.

"And all bustin' with life, both day and night."

"Maybe you could take me there some time," she said.

He shook his head sadly. "There's not much of it left. Not like it was. We've taken more from it than it can regrow on its own."

"Then we'll just enjoy this," she said, laying her head on his shoulder. He liked the feel of it.

"That's good enough for me," he replied, patting her hand.

"Of course," she said, "much as I like the country, I have to admit to preferring the amenities of living in the city."

"And what city do you prefer?"

"Well, there are plenty of them I haven't seen yet," she replied. "And as you well know, I want to, some day.

"But I've already seen a fair number: St. Louis, New Orleans, Kansas City, Denver. They're all nice, in their own ways.

"But honestly, I've never seen one yet that I liked any better than being right here in Fort Rogers."

"It is a pretty nice little place, isn't it?"

"It is. And getting better, I think. Thanks to you, mostly."

"Oh, git on with ya, girl."

"It's true, and you know it."

"Whatever you say, darlin'."

"Wherever it is that I finally settle down for good," she said wistfully, "I'd like to have a house of my very own to live in."

"You've never had that?"

"Only if you count the orphanage where I grew up as a house," she told him. "It sure wasn't a home. And since leaving there, it's mostly been hotel rooms for me."

Jason remembered her telling him about the horrible institution in which she had been abandoned and abused as a child: enduring its horrors until the gambler Cash Carpenter had met her and rescued her from the miserable life she had led within its foreboding walls. The two of them had been a couple ever since.

"And what kinda place would you want this house of yours to be?" he now asked her.

"It would probably sound silly."

"Try me."

"All right. Once, while we were in Denver, Cash and I accepted an invitation to visit a friend of his who had a place away from the city, up in the foothills.

"It was beautiful. It reminded me of descriptions I've read of hunting lodges. Made of stone and large timbers. An enormous fireplace in the main room. Two stories tall. More space than a family of six would need.

"Put me in a house like that...and I'd probably be content to stay there for the rest of my life."

"Then we'll just have to make sure you get that, won't we?" he said lightly.

"Absolutely!"

"And when we do, will I be able to come visit you there?"

"Any time you like," she said, squeezing his arm again. "And stay as long as you want."

"Evenin', folks," a cheerful voice called out to them.

Approaching them from the opposite direction came Copperhead Dick Johnson. He cut almost a dashing figure now in the tan uniform he and the other park guards wore on duty. He also wore a gun strapped to his waist and in his hand carried a short, stout billy club, which he loosely swung back and forth by its wrist strap.

"Dick," Jason greeted him, nodding. "Everything all right, I hope."

"Right as rain. Everything's been nice and quiet of late: and I think I see more people here every night."

"You and your men must be doing a good job," Jane complimented him, bringing a fresh smile to Copperhead's broad face.

"People want nice things, nice places," he said. "Most people, anyway. This lets 'em have it."

His words, unfortunately, were then punctuated by the ominous sound of a gunshot ringing out.

CHAPTER 33

Mankiller threw himself in front of Jane, enveloping her in his arms and pulling her with him down to the ground.

Copperhead joined them even as a second shot sang out. A slug kicked up gravel less than a foot from Jason's head. This time, he was able to see the flash of the gun in the darkness, though not the identity of the shooter.

When no other shots followed for several seconds, he carefully lifted himself off of Jane, who looked stunned.

"Are you all right?" he asked fearfully.

"I think so," she replied, as though not sure.

"Watch out for her, Dick," Jason said as he rose to his feet. "Protect her with your life."

"Word of honor, boss," Copperhead said, also standing.

Still on the ground, Jane plucked at Mankiller's pants leg. "What are you going to do, Jason?"

"What has to be done, darlin'," he replied, smiling down at her tightly before heading out in the direction from which the shots had come.

The drifter didn't wear his gunbelt on such nights out as this, but there was no way he would go about unarmed. He'd had a tailor in town sew a special leather pocket into his jacket: and from it he now pulled his .44.

Ahead of him, vaguely, he could make out the figures of two men fleeing toward the north exit from the park. It was only logical to assume they were the McClure brothers, who had pledged to track him down and kill him.

Knowing he had little chance of hitting either man from this distance and while running, he still snapped off a shot, which was returned by both assassins he was chasing. They continued to do so as they ran, all their shots flying harmlessly high or wide of him.

Out of the park and nearing the northern fringe of town, he managed to draw closer to them, only to see the outlaws heading for the protective cover of a livery stable. He stopped running, so as to be able to take better aim. He fired two shots that chewed wood from around the door frame of the stable, but saw both his targets make it safely into its darkened confines.

Running in a randomly zigzag pattern, Mankiller made it to the livery without drawing any more fire. Pressing himself against the outer wall near the doorway, he listened for any sound of movement.

Hearing nothing, he took the time to quickly eject the spent shells from his revolver and replaced them with fresh rounds. He did so while keeping one eye closed: that way, when he entered the unlit interior of the stable he would still be able to see rather than being virtually sightless until both eyes could adjust to the dimness.

Rather than walk or even run into the building, he dived sideways through the door, rolling as he hit the floor. Still he drew no fire. He lay where he stopped rolling, again listening. This time he did detect a faint rustling sound.

It came from above, in the stable's hayloft.

As quietly as he could, he made his way to the ladder leading up to the loft and began to ascend it. Every few rungs he would stop and listen again. He would also look down over his shoulder for any sign of movement behind or below him. Reaching the top of the ladder, he cautiously poked just enough of his head up to peer into the loft.

With a roar and a flash of light, a bullet sailed his way. The slug bit into the floor directly in front of him: but though it missed flesh and bone, it did kick up straw dust into Mankiller's eyes.

Momentarily blinded, he ducked back down. As he wiped at his stinging eyes, he heard another familiar sound: that made by the hammer of a pistol falling on an empty chamber. Whoever had fired at him was out of bullets.

Though his vision was still impaired, Jason hurled himself up over the top of the ladder and into the loft. Hoping that only one of his would-be killers awaited him, he moved forward even while still wiping at his teary eyes: striving to reach his foe before the man could reload.

He was unable to react in time when the outlaw instead plowed into him with one shoulder, knocking the bounty hunter down.

As he landed heavily on his side, Jason relaxed his grip on the butt of his own weapon. He saw the pistol hit the floor and begin to spin away. He lunged for it, but missed by a fraction of an inch as the revolver sailed out of the loft and fell to the main floor of the stable below.

At a fresh sound, he rolled to his back just in time to brace himself as his attacker landed atop him. At this close distance, Mankiller was able to see it was the younger of the two McClure brothers: Lem.

Jason threw an arm up to fend off the blows the outlaw was attempting to rain down on his head. At the same time, he used his other fist to pound at McClure's exposed side.

These punches took their toll, causing McClure at last to roll off Mankiller and away from the stunning blows to his ribs. As both men struggled to their feet, Jason grabbed McClure by the front of his shirt, spinning him and slinging him into a stack of bundled hay.

McClure shook his head to clear it, then grinned wildly as he looked down and saw a pitchfork lying nearby. Mankiller saw it at almost the same time and made a leap for it.

McClure reached it first.

CHAPTER 34

Mankiller arched his body and threw it back as McClure lunged forward with the pitchfork.

Its tines came just short of piercing Jason's belly, but he again fell to the floor of the loft. McClure followed after him, raising the pitchfork in both hands and driving it downward.

Jason jerked his head to one side: heard the whistle of the fork and felt the point of one tine slide along his right cheek.

He swung his foot, catching McClure at the ankles and knocking his legs out from under him. Jason scurried over and attempted to grab away the pitchfork. He managed to lay his hands on it, but McClure maintained his own grip as the two of them began to roll back and forth.

At last able to gain the top position with sufficient leverage, Mankiller pushed up to a standing position. Not daring to release his hold on the fork, McClure rose with him.

Like straining wrestlers they stood, each trying in vain to wrench the fork away from the hands of the other. Breathing became more ragged and muscles began to tremble from strain.

Jason then surprised McClure by falling backwards, carrying the outlaw with him. As he did, the bounty hunter lifted a foot and planted it in McClure's midsection. As Mankiller hit the floor, he flipped McClure overhead. Helplessly, the outlaw released his grip on the pitchfork.

Loose hay cushioned his fall, and he was able to bound back on his feet before Jason did. The outlaw charged toward him.

Still down on one knee, Mankiller thrust forward with the fork. He felt a strong jolt race down his arms as McClure impaled himself on the tined instrument. The outlaw let out a choked gasp as the barbs entered his stomach.

Eyes glazing, the dying man grasped at his belly even as Mankiller rose to his feet. Still holding the fork, the bounty hunter pushed forward, driving the tines in deeper and sending McClure stumbling back on his heels.

Jason released his hold on the handle of the pitchfork only when he witnessed McClure go sailing over the edge of the loft floor.

Dropping to the floor and peering out over its rims, he saw McClure's body lying unmoving at a twisted angle on the floor below.

He also heard a scurrying noise from the lower rear of the stable, followed by the sound of the building's back doors being violently slammed open.

Jason staggered over to the loft window, gazing down. As he did, he saw a shadowy figure—no doubt that of Nathan McClure—fleeing from the livery. He was running toward a row of cribs sitting at the northernmost edge of the town.

Mankiller hurriedly descended from the loft. Ignoring the lifeless body of Lem McClure, he searched about for his fallen pistol. Finding it, he took the time to make sure it had not sustained any serious damage in the fall before he set out after the older McClure brother.

He now felt he had gained an additional, potentially useful nugget of knowledge about the escapee: he was a coward.

After all, Nathan had to have been cowering in the livery the whole time: yet he had made no attempt to take on Jason alone when the bounty hunter first entered the stable. Nor had he followed up to the loft to render assistance to his besieged brother. His first instinct was not to rush to Lem's side when he fell—but to save his own skin by running.

A good thing to be aware of. But as Jason also well knew...a coward's bullet could kill you just as surely as could one fired by a brave man.

Crouched low to the ground, Mankiller quickly made his way to the nearest in the line of cribs. These flimsy, one-room shacks were used by lower end prostitutes to entertain their clientele, besides serving as homes to these particular soiled doves. Dim lights shining through the windows indicated several of the shacks were currently in use.

The darkness outside the cribs made it difficult for Jason to see his prey. The lustful sounds—genuinely uttered by the men, faked by the soiled doves—made it difficult for him to hear anything untoward.

He slid along the back of the first crib, then hustled across the short open space between it and the next shack. He cautiously repeated this as he made his way down the line.

Reaching the far end of the fourth such crib, he slowly peered around the corner of its back wall.

His body stiffened as a gun boomed from behind him.

CHAPTER 35

Mankiller felt no pain as he spun and fired his own pistol.
Even though he was denied the luxury to aiming carefully, his bullet flew straight and true, slapping into the chest of the man standing less than twenty feet to his rear.

Jason's eyes narrowed: even from this distance and in the dark, he could tell that the man who had lain in ambush for him had already been dead on his feet before the bounty hunter had gotten off his shot.

Nathan McClure tottered on useless legs; eyes and mouth gaping open in stunned surprise. His gun dropped from his hand and he toppled over sideways.

Mankiller's unspoken question was then answered. Standing behind the fallen outlaw was Marshal Clayton Russell: smoking pistol in hand. He had gunned down McClure before the fugitive could do the same to Jason.

"Thanks, Marshal," the drifter said, holstering his .44 as he walked toward the lawman.

"Just doin' my job." From the sound of his voice and the look in his eyes, Jason surmised that the peace officer had not had call to take a life many times before, if ever.

"How'd you come to be here?" he asked Russell, as much to distract his attention from the body lying at his feet as anything.

"Just happenstance, really," the marshal told him. "I was patrolling near the Deadline when I heard the shooting in the park commence, and I came a'runnin'.

"Copperhead told me what had happened, so I set out after you. I found the other McClure boy you'd done in back in the livery; then followed you here.

"You know what happened next."

"You ever killed a man before?" Jason asked.

"Not near so many as you, bounty man," Russell snapped, then lowered his voice. "But one or two, yeah."

"Maybe the reward you collect on 'im will ease your mind a little," Jason said.

"Won't be no reward. Not for me."

"Why not?"

"It's the law. A peace officer can't lay claim to the reward on any criminal he kills or captures within his own jurisdiction."

"That don't seem fair."

"Fair or not, that's the way it is." Russell nudged the body on the ground lightly with his boot. "You can already lay rightful claim to Lem: you might as well take credit for Nathan here, too. No point letting the reward go to waste."

"There's no law that says I couldn't collect the reward and then give it to you, is there, Marshal?"

"None that I know of. But I don't hold to sidestepping the law, neither: so I wouldn't take it."

"And that's all there is to it?"

"That's all there is."

"Then I reckon that's how it'll go." Mankiller now cast a look around. "Is Sheriff Stimson still in town?"

"Yeah. He's probably in his room back at the Hansen House. Why?"

"I just figgered maybe we oughtta pull him in on this. It was his jail that McClure busted out of, after all."

"That's right. And he will wanna know what happened."

"I'll wait here with the body if you want to go fetch him," Jason offered.

The marshal nodded and set out for the hotel. As it happened, Sheriff Stimson was just leaving the dining room as Russell entered the lobby. After a brief recounting of what had transpired, the two men left the hotel together.

Russell showed Stimson the body in the livery stable first, then led him to the spot behind the cribs where the elder McClure had met his violent end.

Only the body was no longer there. And neither was Jason Mankiller.

"I don't understand," Russell muttered.

"Are you sure McClure was dead, Clay?" Stimson asked.

"Dead as a man can get," the marshal avowed.

"Marshal! Sheriff!" Russell's head jerked to the side, recognizing as he did the voice of Mankiller. He could vaguely make out the bounty hunter, standing a good thirty yards away, waving at the two peace officers and calling for them to join him.

Marshall Russell was amazed when they walked over to that spot—and saw the bounty hunter standing over the body of Nathan McClure.

"Did you forget where we were, Marshal?" Mankiller asked.

"Yeah, Clay," Stimson said. "I thought you said you shot McClure right next to one of the cribs."

"He meant not far from one of 'em," Jason said before Russell could utter a sound.

"This is McClure, all right, Sheriff. Check 'im out for yourself."

"I'll just do that, young fella," Stimson said. Kneeling down, he identified the corpse for himself. He noted that, as the marshal had told him, the body had holes in both front and back.

"Give me yer version of what happened, Mankiller," he said as he stood back up.

The drifter proceeded to do so, with the only part of his story differing from that told by Russell being the precise location where the shooting had occurred.

"Looks like it was a righteous killin' to me," Stimson said. "I can't imagine the judge at the inquest will see it any different." He sighed and looked at the bounty hunter.

"After that formality, Mankiller, you can put in a claim for your rewards."

"Just one reward, Sheriff," Jason corrected. "I took out Lem, right enough, but this one belongs to Marshal Russell."

"I'd agree with you, boy: but the law wouldn't. He can't lay claim to the bounty."

"Because the shooting took place within his jurisdiction?"

"That's right."

"The end of his jurisdiction being the city limits of Fort Rogers?"

"Right again."

"Well, now, I'm no expert when it comes to such things—but I think we're outside those limits."

Stimson looked down at the body, back at the cribs at the edge of the city, then over to Marshal Russell.

"Is that right, Clay?"

Russell didn't look at the sheriff. His eyes were bearing down on Mankiller, who guilelessly stared back at him without flinching.

"Looks that way, Aaron," he said at last.

"Good," the sheriff said, slapping his comrade on the back. "Good! You deserve it, and I'll see that you get it.

"I guess that we'd best roust the undertaker and get these two owlhoots taken care of 'fore they spoil."

"Go on ahead, Aaron," Russell said. "I'll be right behind you."

The sheriff took off at a light trot and Jason began to walk in his wake. Russell kept pace with him.

"That was a dirty, low-down trick you pulled, Mankiller," the lawman hissed.

"I got no idea what you're talking about, Marshal."

"The hell you don't!"

"The hell I do." Jason stopped because Russell stopped, right near the spot where the shooting had actually occurred."

"We both know you moved that body!"

"I didn't do no such thing. And even if I did—that don't change the fact that it was you who put McClure under."

The lawman's eyes scoured the ground, pausing when they lit on a patch of darkened dirt that appeared to be stained with blood.

He began to kneel down, but before he could get closer, Mankiller scuffed his boot vigorously back and forth over the dirt, obliterating all sign.

"Listen to me, Russell," Jason said. "We both know the money's rightfully yours. You ain't stealing…just accepting what you've earned."

"Still…"

"Here's something else you might not have thought of. McClure would have killed me sure if you hadn't showed up when you did. So I owe you now. And having a man like me beholden to you might just prove to be a good thing some day."

"That's not why I did it," the peace officer protested.

"I know that. You did it 'cause it was the right thing to do. Just like accepting your share of the reward is the right thing."

"It don't feel right."

"Then give some of it to the poor: I know ya got 'em here in this town. And put the rest in the bank." Jason smiled wickedly. "It'll make your dotage more comfortable."

The marshal growled derisively and stomped away.

CHAPTER 36

Mankiller split off from Marshal Russell as they re-entered the city limits: turning his steps toward the park where he had left Jane.

He found her seated on the edge of one of its benches, her face looking northward, her legs nervously jumping up and down.

Copperhead Johnson, true to his word, stood guard over the woman. The other two guards had joined him, and the three of them had positioned themselves in a circle around the woman.

"You can stand down, Dick," Jason said as he drew near. "Everything's all right now."

Jane leaped to her feet and rushed to hug him tightly. His body seemed to her to be hard and inflexible; and he did not return the embrace with which she welcomed him back.

"I'm gonna see Jane home," the drifter told Johnson, "then prob'ly put myself to bed."

"Yessir," Copperhead said smartly. With a jerk of his head, he directed his two underlings to return to patrolling the park.

Jason accepted Jane's arm in his as he escorted her back toward The Bloody Eye, but he said not a word as they strode down the street, so lost in his own mind was he. The lady gambler was puzzled and increasingly upset by his cool behavior. Only as they paused beneath the glow of a street lamp did she see the cut on his right cheek that had been inflicted by the pitchfork-wielding Lem McClure.

"You're hurt," she said solicitously, reaching up to lightly touch the wound.

His head jerked away as if her gentle touch had burned his flesh. "It's just a scratch," he said brusquely.

By the time they drew near the saloon where their respective rooms were, Jane was seething. She pulled her arm free and moved to plant herself in front of him, blocking his path.

"I've had enough of this," she declared hotly, hands on hips. "What's wrong, Jason?"

"Nothin'."

"Don't tell me that. You've barely spoken to me since we left the park."

"Why don't you just go on inside?" he said, pointedly ignoring her query. "I want to walk around a little bit more before I call it a night."

"Have I done something to upset you?" she pressed him.

"Go on now," he again told her. "If word of the shooting has spread, Cash'll be worried about you."

"He's still locked in with those other high rollers," she countered. "He wouldn't know if the whole rest of the town burned down around him."

"Dammit, would you just do what I tell you, Janie?" Mankiller said, plainly exasperated.

"Not till you talk to me," she said stubbornly.

The bounty hunter stared down at his boots for what seemed to Jane to be several minutes. When he raised his head to look at her, there was a pained expression on his chiseled face.

"I think mebbe it would be best if you stayed away from me from now on."

"...accepting your share of the reward..."

This time it was the woman who stared back at him in silence: in her case, because she was too stunned to speak.

"Did I do something I shouldn't have?" she finally asked when she regained her tongue.

"O' course not."

"Then what is it? What brought this on?"

She saw the distressed look on his face again.

"You could have been killed tonight, Jane."

"So could you."

"But I was their target: I've come to expect that. You'd have just been an innocent bystander. Dead for no other reason than that you were with me."

"That wasn't your fault."

"Yes it was. I've brought it on myself, I know: the life I've chosen to lead makes me a marked man. And it puts anyone close to me in danger, too."

She shook her head. "I deal faro in saloons. A few days ago, I was fighting off Indians. Life comes with danger."

"But there's no need to court it unnecessarily by keeping company with me."

"So what are you going to do—cut yourself off from humanity completely and go live alone in a cave somewhere?"

"Well, no. But –"

"Or are you just saying you want shed of *me*? If this is just an excuse, if it's just because you've grown tired of my company, Jason—have the guts to say so."

He reacted as if she had physically slapped him.

"You know that ain't so, girl."

"No, I don't. All I really know at the moment is that in one minute you've caused me to go from being worried to death about you to being mad enough to soak your head in a horse trough!'

With that, the woman hiked up her skirts slightly and stomped up the steps leading into The Bloody Eye.

Mankiller stayed where he stood, totally confused. He took a step toward the saloon, then thought better of it and took off down the street.

"Havin' female trouble, are ya, Sarge?"

Looking to one side, Jason saw his old Army buddy Theo Hutton. The tobacconist was leaning forward over the cross rail of a hitching post, leisurely puffing away at a pipe.

"What brings you out here, Theo?" Mankiller asked.

"Same as you, sorta. Guess I was gettin' underfoot, so the missus run me off: told me not ta come back home for at least an hour."

Jason approached the post, shaking his head slowly. "I think it's gonna take more than an hour for Jane to cool off."

"Aw, she'll get over whatever wound it was you inflicted on 'er," Hutton said. "Just as soon as *you've* suffered enough."

Jason chuckled softly. "How'd a gimpy-legged corporal get to be so smart about such things?"

"Mostly by learnin' from the bad example set by sergeants."

Hutton removed the pipe from between his teeth, frowning slightly as he saw the fire had almost completely gone out of it.

"I know my Sally has sure took a shine to ya, Sarge. She's already after me to have you back ta supper again."

"Tell her that'd be a pure-dee pleasure. What that woman can do with not much more than a plain old squirrel is nothing short of magic."

"Yeah, she's had ta learn how ta make do with whatever comes ta hand. She's known mighty lean times in her life: before we were married, and sometimes after."

"But things are all right for you 'n' her and the children now, aren't they?"

"Couldn't be better. Moving here and opening up my own business is the best thing that's happened ta us in years. And don't think me and her don't thank God 'n' you ever' day for it, Sarge."

"I didn't do so much."

"You surely did. Starting with saving my life, back there in the Wilderness. Sharing a measly squirrel dinner with ya don't begin ta pay you back for all you've done." He gave Mankiller a crooked grin.

"No wonder Sally loves you damn near as much as she does me!"

"You got you a good one there, corporal," Jason said earnestly.

"Don't I know it. 'Course, that Jane o' yers is a swell gal, too, near as I can see."

Now it was Mankiller who frowned. "No. It's not like that with me and her."

"Then how is it?"

"We're friends, that's all. Good friends."

"Does she know that's all you are?"

"Absolutely. She's committed to that man of hers, Cash Carpenter; as well she should be."

"He's that flashy gambler, hangs out at The Bloody Eye, ain't he?"

"That's him. And that's all there is to it."

Knowing when his former sergeant was closing the door on a subject, yet not fully willing to let this cat loose, Hutton eyed the drifter.

"What about the little Mex gal you brung ta town?"

"Rosario? She's a good friend, too."

"How good?"

Jason bristled slightly. "I make it a habit not to talk too loosely about womenfolk, corporal."

"Uh-huh. That's a habit more men oughtta get into, I s'pose." The tobacconist paused before pressing on anyway.

"Word is you brought her little girl along with ya when you called on Sarah Applegate Sunday last."

Mankiller made no effort to hide his annoyance. "What are you, Theo— the town gossip?"

"It's true, ain't it?"

"Mostly. Little Anita's new here: she ain't had time to make any friends yet. And children need other children. She got on real well with Toby and his sisters."

"And you got along real well with the mama."

"That woman's had a rough row to hoe, old son. She deserves a good turn."

"Yeah, well, all's I'm sayin' is you got half the town thinkin' yer a Mormon." Hutton wagged a finger. "And that ain't even countin' all them Mex laundry women. Why, any one of 'em would take up with you in a heartbeat. And that's just in *this* town."

Jason snorted.

"In fact," Theo continued, "I think that may just be yer *real* problem, Sarge."

"What's that?" Jason said, knowing he was going to hear the answer whether he wanted to or not.

"You got more women on your hands than Solomon would know what ta do with!"

Mankiller didn't want to, but at this he couldn't stop himself from laughing aloud. Hutton joined in, practically cackling at his own observation.

Winding down, the bounty hunter exhaled wearily. "Y'know, this is one of those occasions when I think I'd like to succumb to temptation and indulge in a nice cold beer. I'd be glad to stand you to one if you'd care to join me, Theo."

Hutton turned his pipe over, tapping it lightly against the hitching rail to dislodge the few smoldering remnants of tobacco from its bowl.

"Sometimes, you can be downright persuasive, Sarge."

"Yeah? Tell that to Jane."

CHAPTER 37

Cash Carpenter stood on the sidewalk outside the front doors of The Bloody Eye saloon, sipping at a mug of beer.

Its cold and somewhat bitter bite cut through the slight, raspy dryness of his throat; which had been brought on by inhaling too much cigar and cigarette smoke from inside the saloon over the past several days.

He squinted slightly in the sunlight, as it had been awhile since last he saw its full glare. The marathon poker game in which he had been engaged had finally broken up just a few hours ago.

Cash had not been the biggest winner—that honor went to a dapper gent by the name of Ben Short out of Austin—but his purse was at least a little fuller and heavier than it had been at the start of the game.

About half a block away, he spotted Jane Starr and Jason Mankiller. Jason was mounted on his buckskin: both man and beast looked far healthier than they had upon their arrival in Fort Rogers. Jane was standing beside the horse, looking up at and speaking with its rider. The conversation didn't appear to be an angry one, but it was certainly animated.

From this distance, Cash couldn't hear any of what they were saying; but finally he saw Jane reach up and take Jason's hand, squeezing it and pressing it to her cheek.

Mankiller tipped his hat to her and reined the buckskin around, riding it at a walk toward Carpenter; bringing the horse to a halt as he came abreast of the gambler.

"You're not leaving town already, are you, Jason?"

"Yep. I got some unfinished business to take care of."

"I was hoping we'd have more time."

"Why's that?"

"Because I don't feel like I've adequately shown you my appreciation for saving me and Jane from the depredations of our Comanche brethren."

"A simple thanks'll do, Cash."

"That hardly seems sufficient payment for my life and hers."

"You don't owe me a blessed thing, pardner. After all, you've helped pull my ashes outta the fire a time or two."

"I still don't feel like our tallies have evened out."

Mankiller rose up slightly off his saddle, stretching his back. "There is one favor you could do for me, Cash: one that would wipe the slate clean as far as I'm concerned."

"Name it," Carpenter said without hesitation.

Jason looked back over his right shoulder to make sure Jane wasn't watching them. She had her back to the pair, strolling down the street in the opposite direction (so as not to have to watch his leaving? he wondered).

"I want you to take Jane to New York City."

"You're running us out of town?" Cash jested, though his expression showed he was somewhat surprised by the request.

"No, of course not," Jason replied, smiling wryly. "I just mean for a visit. Bright lights…big city. Give the lady a chance to see the elephant."

"You really think that's something she's eager to do?"

Now it was Jason who was a bit surprised. "Hasn't she told you so?"

"I suppose," the gambler said, staring down at his boots. "I believe she did say something about wanting to meet her publisher."

"There ya go. And while she's doing that—you can find out if gamblers back East are as easy for you to honey-fuggle as the ones here in the West are."

Cash grinned, obviously relishing that prospect.

"Just be sure you tear yourself away from the gaming tables long enough to take our girl out on the town. Show her the sights; take her out dancing and to the theater. Wine and dine her. Do that for me, wouldja?"

"I'd be delighted."

Jason leaned over sideways in the saddle and slipped a thick fold of cash into one of the gambler's coat pockets.

"A little something to get you started," he said. "Just between us."

"I couldn't –" Cash protested, looking down again to withdraw the money from his pocket.

When he did, Mankiller put his heels to the buckskin and took off down the street.

Shaking his head, Cash smiled slightly and slid the money back into his coat before stepping down from the sidewalk and setting out after Jane.

Behind him, Jason slowed down his horse, then brought it to a stop as he saw Marshal Russell step out onto the street and wave him down.

Russell noted that the bounty hunter appeared to be freshly equipped. The saddle on his mount shined with new leather: its saddlebags bulged slightly with supplies. Resting in a scabbard on its right side was a new Henry lever-action repeating rifle.

"Heading out, are you?" the lawman asked.

"I am. That should make you happy."

"Don't make me nothin'," Russell said gruffly. "Just curious, that's all."

Jason noticed the marshal was holding a copy of the *Diligence* in one hand. "Checking out the news, are you, Marshal?"

"Huh? Oh," Russell said, having forgotten he was holding the paper. "Naw. Looking in the ads. Now that it looks like I'm gonna be making a little more money, I'm thinking of maybe finding better lodgings for myself."

Jason nodded. "You might consider the widow Pennington's boarding house."

"Nice place, is it?"

"Real nice. Clean, too. Good neighborhood: reasonable rates."

"I'll look into it."

"Mmm." Jason shrugged. "If you end up taking a room there," he nonchalantly added, "would you mind keeping an eye on Rosario Mendoza and her little one?"

"That the woman you rode into town with? The one who runs the new restaurant?"

"The same."

"I reckon I could do that."

"I'd be obliged." Mankiller turned his face away from the lawman and stared into the distance.

"Marshal...I'm sorry I spilled blood in your town again."

"Weren't your fault, boy: you was defending yourself. I'd just as soon it never happened again, though."

Jason kept his eyes averted. "Does that mean you're posting me outta town?" He envisioned a life in exile.

"I thought about it," Russell said gruffly.

"Can't say as I'd blame ya."

"There's plenty here now who would, though. Whether you know it or not, you've made a fair number of friends here, son." The rugged lawman momentarily averted his eyes. "I might even be one of 'em."

"That's good to know."

"Just don't ever let these people down."

"I'll do my best not to. I've kinda took a shine to this place."

"So, does that mean you're planning on coming back?"

"God willin' and the creek don't rise," the drifter replied lightly.

"Or some malcontent don't put a bullet in your back."

"Would that bother you, Marshal?"

"Wouldn't make me no never mind one way or t'other."

"Uh-huh."

"You hear that?" Russell asked, again turning his eyes from the bounty hunter. The sound of pounding hammers and grinding saws hung heavy in the air.

"Sounds like there's some construction going on," Jason commented.

"That's exactly what it is. Couple of new buildings, I hear. From what I've been told, one of 'em's gonna be a new apothecary that Doc Crotty and his wife plan to run."

"That's progress for you, I guess," Jason sighed.

"You don't sound too happy about it, son."

"Just wondering if too much civilizing might be a bad thing."

"Mebbe so," Russell mused. "But I reckon I'll be dead before things get too tame."

"Me, too, Marshal," Mankiller said, then made a snicking sound with his tongue against his teeth to urge his mount forward.

The lawman removed his hat and scratched his head as he watched the drifter ride away. It puzzled him greatly that a bounty killer would harbor such soft feelings.

Mankiller passed the lot where the Mexican women did laundry. They were going about their chores as usual, even though some of the construction work Marshal Russell had mentioned was going on all around them.

Through Byron Longfellow, Jason had purchased the lot and was paying for the erection of a building that would eventually form a real laundry; one that would have running water and protect the ladies from the elements. The bounty hunter was also responsible for the building of the apothecary that would be attached to Dr. Crotty's medical office.

When he'd shared a table with Sarah Applegate and her children, Mankiller hadn't bothered to mention to the woman that he had instructed Longfellow to offer her the position of proprietor of the laundry once construction was finished. He and Longfellow had agreed that having the bounty hunter's name attached to the enterprise would guarantee that both Sarah and the laundresses under her would have a decent work environment and receive fair recompense for the service they provided.

He tipped his hat to the smiling ladies as he rode by, but he didn't stop.

At the western edge of town, the drifter came to Rosario's Restaurant. His eyes narrowed as he gazed at the new sign that had been installed above the front entrance.

In the lower right corner of the sign had been painted a smaller rendition of the same bleeding eye that adorned Sam Dobbin's re-dubbed saloon.

The exact small symbol, always in the same spot, now adorned the signs of the Hansen House and the Grand Comique. He had no doubt this emblem would also find its way onto the signage of the future laundry and apothecary shop.

No amount of complaining on Jason's part could convince Sam to remove this symbol; it was good for business, the older man insisted. Mankiller had finally given up his protest as being a lost cause. He no doubt could have compelled his partner to give in: but the affection he held for the crusty saloonkeeper who had given him work when he was down and out prevented him from doing so.

The drifter walked his buckskin around the building and then he entered the restaurant through its back door. This led into the kitchen, where Rosario Mendoza was working over a large stove. Her daughter sat on the floor out of the way, playing with her puppy.

"Mmm-hmm," he intoned. "Somethin' smells good."

"Senor Jason!" Anita squealed, jumping to her feet and running over to throw her arms around his legs.

"What brings you here?" Rosario asked, brushing back a wisp of hair that had fallen out of place over her forehead.

"I'll be gone on business for awhile, and I just wanted to stop by and say so long to two of my favorite girls before I left."

A concerned look crossed Rosario's face; she knew well what his "business" entailed. He looked away from her as he felt Anita tug at his belt.

"Can I ask you a question?" Her tiny voice barely reached him.

"Sure you can, sweetheart."

"Do you kill people?" she asked calmly.

The child's mother gasped in shock, and Jason dropped down to one knee to put himself down on Anita's level.

"Why would you ask me that, child?" he said gently.

"Toby Applegate told me you kill people. Do you?"

He desperately looked up at Rosario, but her stricken expression told him she had nothing to offer by way of getting him out of this.

"I'd never kill anybody who wasn't a bad man," he assured the little girl.

"So you won't kill *me*, will you?"

"Oh, dear Lord, no!" he moaned, throwing his arms around the child and pulling her close to him.

"You're my little chickabiddy. I'd never do anything to hurt you!"

"Okay," she said, instantly accepting his answer unquestioningly. She gave him a big kiss on the cheek, then looked over at her mother.

"Can me and Hector go outside and play now?"

A stunned Rosario could only nod mutely and watch as child and dog ran out the door together.

"I'm so sorry, Jason," she finally said, in a voice barely above a whisper.

"It wasn't your fault," he replied numbly, rising to his feet with his head hung low. Then he looked up at the woman.

"What about you, Rosario? Are you scared of me?"

"Oh, no!" she exclaimed, her hand flying to her mouth. "No...no. And neither is Anita. You saw that."

"That's good," he said, turning his head to watch the little girl and her pooch romping out back. "That's good." He sighed deeply.

"Still," he continued, turning back to Rosario, "I'd understand if you didn't want me to come around you and the little one no more."

At this, the woman's features twisted in what he perceived to be anger.

"Jason Mankiller—what's wrong with you?" she snapped, swatting him with a wet dishtowel she had been holding. He flinched—only from surprise, as there was no actual physical pain—even as she swatted him again.

"That little girl out there loves you! So don't you even *think* about breaking her heart by leaving her for good!"

"No, ma'am," he said, grinning crookedly now as he threw up an arm to ward off yet another swat from the dishtowel.

"Where are you going?" she demanded as he began to back out of the door.

"I'm leaving town for awhile, remember?"

"Oh, get back in here and sit down," she growled, "while I fix you some food to take with you."

"Yes, ma'am," he said meekly, doffing his hat and taking a seat on a stool.

"Some killer you are!" Rosario huffed, starting to stuff tortillas with beans, peppers and strips of grilled chicken.

Jason smiled again.

CHAPTER 38

Mankiller had waited until the sun went down before riding into the sleepy little town of Rio Caballo.

He was too easily recognized; and in a town this small, anyone who saw him might be a friend of Rodrigo Chavez and so inclined to tell him about the tattooed stranger who'd just come to town. So he needed to be careful about how he sought information on the Comanchero.

Jason rode slowly all the way through the hamlet along its short main street: staying in the shadows and pulling his hat down low over his face.

His eyes moved from side to side constantly; getting the lay of the land, seeking out places that would be the most likely sources for intelligence.

There were a couple of cantinas in town, and he drew close to the one that outwardly appeared to be the seediest and most disreputable.

He didn't enter the place, but planted himself outside a side window, having chosen a spot that was in the dark and then surveyed the interior of the establishment.

The bar was nothing more than a few rough-hewn boards laid across the tops of some empty barrels: its floor nothing more than packed dirt.

It catered to an equally rough-looking clientele: both Mexicans and Anglos. None of them there at the moment was either Chavez or the other two Comancheros with whom he sometimes rode.

The bounty hunter's sharp eyes quickly settled on an older man who clearly needed liquor badly and just as clearly didn't have the money to pay for it. Those whom he tried to beg a drink from either ignored him or roughly cuffed him away.

It seemed obvious that he was a *barrel boarder*—a sot—and one that was already thoroughly roostered.

Finally growing tired of the bum pestering his other patrons, the bartender grabbed the lush by the back of his collar and the seat of his pants and hustled him toward the front doors. He roughly shoved the bum through the batwings so hard that the man staggered off the edge of the sidewalk and fell hard to the dirt street beyond.

The sot managed to stagger back up on his feet and climb up onto the sidewalk. He attempted to walk away with as much dignity as he could muster; but the toe of a boot caught the edge of a warped board and he again took a nasty fall.

This time, he just stayed where he lay.

Having witnessed all this, Mankiller quickly moved to where his horse was tethered and removed a bottle of rotgut whiskey from his saddlebags.

He had packed three such bottles before leaving Fort Rogers, anticipating that his hunt might bring him into contact with Indians (tame or otherwise) or half-breeds: to whom such might be an inducement to render him assistance or provide him with information.

Still hugging the shadows, he pulled the fallen bum back up on his feet; and then half-carried him well away from the cantina and other nearby buildings.

After propping the stuporous old man up against a tree in a sitting position, Jason uncorked his whiskey bottle and splashed a little of its contents on his face and neck like cologne; so as to create the illusion that he too had been drinking heavily.

He found himself appreciating the fact that the smell of the alcohol in his nostrils would help mask the cacophony of foul odors emanating from the drunk: it was the blended aroma of unwashed flesh, vomit and urine. Added to the mix was the scent of some of the horse manure the hopeless wretch had wallowed in out on the street.

At least, Jason hoped it was simply horse manure.

He lightly slapped the old man to bring him partially to his senses. The sot's eyes fluttered open: the pale pupils nearly invisible against the bloodshot whites.

"Who are you?" the lush said suspiciously. "Wadda ya want?"

"I'm a friend," Jason assured him.

The sot snorted. "Ain't got no friends."

"Sure you do. You got me."

"Oh." The old man tried in vain to focus his eyes. He had no idea where he was, or who Jason was—but he recognized the contents of the bottle his new "friend" was holding. He smacked his lips loudly.

"Friends share," he whined.

"So they do," Jason replied, offering up the bottle. "Have a swig."

After taking a long, loud pull on the bottle, the drunk cradled it in his arms like a baby, making no effort to return it to his benefactor.

"How come yer bein' so nice?" He began to slide over sideways until Mankiller grabbed him and straightened him back up.

"'Cause I seen how bad them other fellas was treatin' you back in the cantina," Jason sympathized, affecting a slurred manner of speech.

"I been mistreated too, friend," he said pointedly. "'Specially by that no-good Rodrigo Chavez."

"Shhh!" the drunk warned, raising a shaking finger to his cracked lips. The name Jason had intoned seemed to cut a little through the man's stupor.

"That there Mex is plumb no good," he told Jason. "He'd just as soon cut yer heart out as look at ya." He took another deep gulp from the bottle.

"Don't take much ta git on his bad side, neither. Particularly if he thinks yer gettin' a mite too friendly with Bonita."

"Who's Bonita?"

"You know Bonita, mister," the sot insisted. "Ever'body knows Bonita. She's that damned swish-ass *puta* Chavez favors."

"Oh, yeah," Jason said. "She lives in a room up over the cantina, don't she?"

"Nooo," the old sot scoffed. "Yer thinkin' o' Esperanta."

"Oh."

"Yeah. Bonita's the one lives in the little shack at the southern outskirts o' town. The one with the gray slate roof."

"Right, right. 'Course, if Chavez ain't around, he don't know what his puta might be up to, eh?" Jason chuckled and poked the sot lightly in the ribs with an elbow.

The old man giggled in response, then heaved a sigh. "Trouble is, the bastard *is* here. He's prob'ly with 'er right now."

Mankiller grinned wolfishly at his good fortune.

"Oh, well…there's always tomorrow, eh?"

The old drunk giggled again.

Figuring he'd gotten all he needed from the sot, Jason reached out and pushed the whiskey bottle up toward the old man's mouth.

"Drink up, friend," he said, "while I go fetch us a fresh bottle."

"You do that."

Casting off the pretense of inebriation, Mankiller walked away. He was certain that the old man would finish off the current bottle, pass out and likely remember neither the drifter nor their conversation.

After stopping at a public horse trough to wash away the stink of booze and bum, the bounty hunter mounted and easily found his way to the house of the prostitute named Bonita. In actuality, it would be more accurate to call it a crib: tiny and probably consisting of no more than a single room. The kind of place where women like Bonita both lived and worked.

On the ground beneath the shack's single window sat a small, forlorn clay pot from which a few pale flowers sprouted: an effort, at least, to bring a little beauty to the ugly crib.

Seeing a horse tethered in front of the small shack, Mankiller dismounted and stealthily moved forward on foot. No light shone from within the place; nor could the drifter detect any noise coming from within when he pressed an ear to the flimsy front door.

Finding the portal to be unlocked, he slowly and silently eased it open, entering the shack with pistol in hand.

Only to be struck in the back of the head by something hard and heavy!

CHAPTER 39

By sheer happenstance, the whore called Bonita had been out back behind the crib, making use of the privy, when Mankiller had approached her domicile. She had returned from conducting her personal business just in time to see the bounty hunter entering the house.

With one hand clutching the sheet that was all that was covering her nakedness, she had used the other hand to snatch up her solitary flower pot and wielded it to club the intruder in the back of the head.

As Jason staggered forward, dropping his pistol, Bonita stepped on her sheet, tripping herself. The sheet flew off as she fell into the bounty hunter; and both of them toppled onto the edge of the crib's single bed—spilling a groggy, sleep-and-booze clouded Rodrigo Chavez atop them on the floor.

All three of them became entangled in flailing arms and legs—and the flapping folds of Bonita's sheet.

With no illumination save the pale beam of moonlight coming in through the open door, Jason was just able to make out that Chavez had managed to lay a hand on what was apparently his weapon of choice: a large and wicked-looking bowie knife.

Still absent his fallen pistol, Mankiller frantically clawed for the skinning knife riding on the right side of his gunbelt. He pulled it free just as the Mexican threw himself atop the drifter.

With each man desperately gripping the other's wrist, they rolled along the floor. When they slammed into a wall, Jason jerked free and tumbled away: Chavez's flashing knife blade barely missing him and thunking into the floor.

Both combatants sprang to their feet and warily circled: looking for an advantage. Chavez lunged forward, hoping to sink his blade into the bounty hunter's belly. Mankiller twisted aside while swinging his own knife. He heard a grunt and saw a dark gash appear high on the Mexican's chest.

He and Chavez charged each other like enraged bulls: slamming together and again grabbing each other's wrist. As they strained for leverage, the woman bounded around them hysterically, assailing Mankiller with a fiery stream of obscene Spanish invectives.

Chavez felt himself slowly losing ground, being pushed back until his back was to the wall. As his foe pressed closer, the moonlight allowed him to see the man's face clearly for the first time: revealed the unmistakable red teardrop tattoo.

The Comanchero began to sweat even more profusely as the irrational part of his brain wondered if he was being attacked by some ghoul risen from the dead; for surely the man Chavez had helped deliver into the clutches of the Comanches could not still be alive!

With a wild scream, the naked Bonita leaped through the air, landing on Mankiller's back. As her arms and legs wrapped around him, she sank her teeth into the lobe of his right ear.

Yelling in pain, Jason released his grip on Chavez. The outlaw pulled free and lunged forward with his bowie. To this point, Mankiller had only suffered minor nicks and cuts, but now he felt the blade slice through his shirt and rake sharply along his side.

He spun wildly, still carrying the woman on his back, slamming her into Chavez. Again, all three of them hit the floor in a pile.

Finding his booted foot pressed up against Bonita's belly, Jason straightened his leg fiercely, sending the soiled dove winging away from him.

Chavez had rolled up into a crouch and, seeing an opening, sprang toward the bounty hunter. As he did, Mankiller lunged at him, knife blade extended before him.

Unable to stop or turn, the Comanchero impaled himself on the point of the skinning knife.

Jason's left hand shot up to grip Chavez behind his head, clamping down and holding him in place while insinuating the blade of his knife even deeper into the Comanchero's chest cavity. When steel met heart—steel won.

Chavez was dead by the time Mankiller rolled clear of his body and extracted the blade.

With a strangled cry, certain that she would be the next to die, Bonita raced for the door of her crib, unmindful of her nudity.

Before she could reach it, Mankiller's fingers twined in her wildly flowing hair, snapping her retreat sharply and jerking her backwards. He kicked her feet out from under her and she crashed painfully to the floor.

Jason dropped heavily atop her. Her flaring hips and swelling breasts held no allure for him. Any thought she may have had of screaming for help disappeared when the bounty hunter pressed her head down with one hand while bringing the blade of his skinning knife to her throat.

Mankiller had hoped to take Chavez alive, so as to extract information from him, but the murderous outlaw had taken that option away from him. He hoped now that the whore would serve his needs just as well.

"I want to know about the men Chavez rides with," he hissed menacingly. "Keeler and the half-breed—where can I find them?"

"I don't know!" Bonita professed. "I don't know nothin' about what he does when he's not here!"

"Then I guess you're no use to me, woman," Mankiller snarled, pressing his blade up under her chin hard enough to draw blood.

The whore began to cry uncontrollably, begging for her life between racking sobs. But the cold fire in Mankiller's icy blue eyes told her that neither tears nor pleas for mercy would soften his heart.

"I'll give you a choice," he told her, his lips close to her ear.

"You can be buried in the same hole as Chavez—or in a grave of your own. Decide!" His knife bit deeper into the soft flesh of her neck.

"No!" she blubbered. "I'll tell you all I know!"

"Then do it quick, *puta*," he demanded.

"A…a few days ago. The half-breed; he was here."

"This fella have a name?"

"Pablo Red Wing," she said. "While he was here…Chavez shared me with him." Her lips twisted.

"The man is a filthy pig," she bitterly declared.

"No worse than you deserve, I s'pect," Mankiller said scornfully. "What's become of him?"

"He left: two days ago. When he did, he told Rodrigo to rendezvous with him and Keeler at a place called Desert Bluff."

"So why was Chavez still here?"

The whore almost smiled. "He still had plenty of *dinero* left from his last job—and he likes what I can do for him. So he was in no hurry to leave Rio Caballo." The almost-smile faded.

"That's the truth," she swore. "That's all I know."

The terrified expression on her face was enough to convince Jason that this was so.

The smartest thing to do now, he knew, was to go ahead and slit the woman's throat and be done with it. But hard a man as he was, he lacked that degree of cold-bloodedness. Still, he didn't want her telling others that he was on the trail of the other two Comancheros. Not yet.

"I'll make you a deal, Bonita."

"What sort of deal?"

"The kind that'll let you keep your life. When I leave here, I'll take Chavez's body with me and dispose of it where no one is likely to ever find it or be able to connect it to you."

"Yes!" she said eagerly, seeing a glimmer of hope for her own survival.

"From what I know," Jason continued, "everyone 'round here will be too happy to see Chavez gone to ask any questions of you. But if they do, you just tell 'em he took off in the night to rejoin his compadres."

Bonita silently nodded as much as the knife still at her throat would allow.

"In return for your silence, I'll let you live. And you can keep for yourself anything of value you find in Chavez's clothes and saddlebags."

The greedy light that now replaced the fear in the whore's eyes told Jason he'd made a deal in which she would abide; at least for a time.

But just to be on the safe side, and to seal the bargain, he lightly flicked her ear lobe in payment for the bite she had taken out of his; just enough to draw a few drops of blood and to elicit a squeaky cry of pain.

"You renege on our deal, puta," he threatened, "and I'll come back and finish the job."

"I won't...I swear to God."

Mankiller wasn't sure how God felt, but the bounty hunter himself paid no heed to her vow. He had no doubt that before long the soiled dove would feel compelled to blabber out the story of what had transpired; and of how she had miraculously escaped death at the hand of the Man Who Cries Blood.

That was fine with him; it was actually a good thing for people to know that those who wronged him would be made to pay a heavy price.

He just didn't want word of this to reach Chavez's compatriots before the bounty hunter did.

After retrieving his pistol, Mankiller managed to lift the dead weight that was Chavez and slung him over one shoulder. The drifter hadn't yet reached the door of the crib when he heard a rustling sound behind him.

He made no attempt to hide the look of contempt on his face when he turned to see Bonita, unashamed in her nakedness, already furiously rifling through her dead lover's belongings.

CHAPTER 40

The sun was setting as Mankiller made his way up the sloping side of Desert Bluff.

He stopped short of the top, so as not to present a profile that might be seen by others: dismounting and walking his way to the crest.

He knelt to examine the ground for sign; and even in the faint light he could easily see the earth had been chewed up by the passage of many hooves. He looked first to the north; he thought he recognized this land as being the southern end of the range of a fairly substantial spread called the 2-B.

Looking then to the south, he could just make out, some miles distant, clouds of dust rising up.

His interpretation of what this signified was simple. Keeler and Red Wing had rustled a small herd of cattle, which they probably intended to run down to Mexico and sell.

Remounting, he urged his buckskin on, knowing it would make better speed than could a herd of cantankerous cattle.

He caught up with the herd late on the following afternoon; but stayed back from it at a safe distance.

With the aid of a small spyglass he had packed in his saddlebags, he carefully scouted out the situation facing him.

Through the dust stirred up by the slowly moving herd, Jason could make out the forms of at least four riders pushing it along. Doubtless Keeler and Red Wing had recruited more of their Comanchero cohorts besides Rodrigo Chavez.

The bounty hunter also used the spyglass to scout out the terrain that lay ahead of the rustlers: devising a plan of action accordingly.

He circled wide around the herd, pushing his buckskin hard so as to put himself ahead of the stolen cattle. He maintained a safe distance between them until, near sundown, he saw that the Comancheros were planning to bed their small herd down for the night in a shallow gully.

Dismounting, Mankiller uncinched but did not unsaddle his horse. Hobbling the buckskin, he removed the bit from its mouth to allow it to crop at the sparse shoots of grass at hand.

Before long, he saw the glow of a campfire coming from the outlaw's location; but he maintained a cold camp for himself: lighting no fire. Supper for him consisted of nothing but jerky and hardtack, washed down

"In return for your silence, I'll let you live."

with water. Lying down behind a concealing bush, he quickly fell into a light but restful sleep.

His internal clock woke him around midnight, fully alert. Walking, he led the buckskin closer to the outlaws' camp. Securely tethering the horse to a mesquite, he moved nearer still on foot.

Staying downwind of the cattle as best he could, Mankiller silently scouted the terrain. As far as he could determine, there were only two men riding night herd, keeping guard over the milling steers.

These were the men he needed to take out first.

The bounty hunter waited patiently, watching for any pattern the riders had as they each circled half the herd. He soon discovered that one rustler's route took him near a certain mesquite tree.

Mankiller waited until the rider was well toward the opposite side of his path, then crawled to the mesquite and clambered up its trunk. The soil here was fairly well irrigated and had allowed the mesquite to grow to a height of nearly twenty feet. Jason settled in, lying flat against one of the tree's lower limbs.

Again he would call on the lethal services of his skinning knife: drawing it from its sheath and waiting for the night rider to again pass beneath the spreading branches of the tree.

The rustler's eyes were on the milling cattle, not up in the trees, so he rode slowly directly beneath Mankiller's perch without seeing the drifter. Jason waited till the Comanchero was nearly past him, then dropped down out of the mesquite.

He had timed his leap perfectly, spreading his legs and landing on the horse's rump right behind the rustler. At the sudden, unexpected weight on its back, the startled horse tried to bolt.

Its rider needed both hands on the reins to try to keep his mount under control. This allowed Mankiller freedom to reach around with his left hand, clamping it over the stunned outlaw's mouth to prevent an outcry. This in turn also gave him leverage to pull the rider's head back, exposing his throat.

With a single, deft slash, the bounty hunter slit the Comanchero's throat from ear to ear. Jason felt hot blood spilling out of the wound and over his fingers, along with the rustler's life essence.

Holding tight till he was sure the outlaw was dead, Jason then dumped the body out of the saddle. As it fell, he snatched the sombrero from the rustler's head, slapping it onto his own crown.

His attack had unavoidably caused a certain amount of noise, mostly in the form of the snorting and stamping of the Comanchero's horse. It was still skittish: made more so by the smell of fresh blood disturbing its flared nostrils.

With a firm hand on the reins, Jason held it in check. Leaning forward, he stroked the animal's neck and whispered soothingly in its ear. It was but a matter of moments before he had it completely under his control.

As he had anticipated, though, the second night herder had heard some of the noise—especially that caused by the frightened horse—and was now riding closer to investigate. Mankiller raised a hand to him, signaling that all was well. The darkness and the concealment of the sombrero fooled the Comanchero: he waved back in acknowledgment and resumed his own route around the herd.

For a time, Jason did the same. He softly crooned a wordless tune as he circled the cattle; so as to calm any whom might have grown nervous from the disturbance his attack on the rustler had caused. The last thing the bounty hunter wanted was to do anything that might cause the herd of beeves to stampede. His own experiences as a *vaquero* had taught him how deadly such an occurrence could be.

With the two nightriders each traveling in a half circle around the herd, they inevitably drew somewhat close to each other at the opposing ends of their individual circuits. With slow deliberation, Mankiller made sure that each time he rode closer still to the other herder: so gradually that the rustler did not grow suspicious.

At last, they drew close enough for Jason to make his next move.

To maintain the concealment of his true identity, he slumped forward in his saddle, keeping his head down. So far did he slouch that the other rider thought he might have dozed off.

"Wake up, Diego," the Comanchero whispered loudly.

Mankiller jerked and shook himself slightly, as if he was indeed being roused from slumber.

"This is dull work," he grumbled in Spanish, hoping the sleepy tone he was affecting would disguise his voice also. "I wish I had a good, stiff drink: that would keep me awake."

"I agree," the Comanchero replied, chuckling softly. His voice then took on a conspiratorial timbre. "And I might be able to satisfy that craving—if you don't tell anyone."

"Who'm I gonna tell," Jason muttered, "these cows?"

The other rider chuckled again. "I have a little something in my saddlebags that I'd be willing to share."

As he twisted in his saddle to dig into his bags, Mankiller drew ever closer. When he came abreast of the Comanchero, he launched himself from his saddle: hitting the rustler and tackling him off his mount. Both men hit the ground heavily.

Recovering quickly, the rustler grasped for his pistol. He managed to draw it, but Jason grabbed the man's right wrist. He was still hoping to keep this struggle as quiet as possible, so he had only his knife in his own right hand: but the Comanchero had likewise latched onto his wrist.

The two men rolled back and forth on the ground, wrestling for leverage. Mankiller was nearly as concerned that the Comanchero would get off a wild shot—alerting his cohorts and perhaps stampeding the herd—as he was that the outlaw might actually put a bullet in him.

As their tumbling momentarily put Jason on top, he found himself looking down at the Comanchero's face: its features twisted in a blend of anger and fear. Seeing an opening, the bounty hunter raised his head and slammed it down, butting his foe.

Blood bubbled from the rustler's nose and his hand fell away from Mankiller's wrist. The bounty hunter struck with his knife, driving its blade into the outlaw's ribcage: an action he repeated several times.

Panting for breath, inhaling deeply to draw air into his lungs, Jason rose unsteadily to his feet.

Barely had he done so than he heard a loud crack; followed by a searing pain along the side of his neck that spun him around and slammed him back to the ground.

CHAPTER 41

Clamping his left hand over the wound that was pumping blood from the side of his throat, Mankiller drew his pistol and pushed himself upright.

As he rose, he caught sight of Pedro Red Wing. The half-breed had heard the commotion coming from the fringes of the herd and ridden out to investigate. From atop his horse, he raised his pistol to take a second shot at the interloper.

With no time to bring his own gun to bear, Jason again threw himself on the ground and began to roll. He barely dodged stomping hooves as more shots rang out, plowing up the earth around him.

After rolling several feet farther, the bounty hunter jumped to his feet.

By the time Red Wing spotted him and began to swivel in his direction, Mankiller had assumed his familiar sideways gunfight stance and was taking aim with his Colt.

The pistol barked twice: both slugs striking the Comanchero's chest squarely in the center.

The half-breed swayed for a moment in the saddle, his brain slow to realize what his lifeless body already knew. His hand lowered, and as he pitched over the side of his saddle a last convulsive spasm triggered his pistol.

The gun discharged, its slug flying harmlessly into the dirt—but not before it sizzled its way along the right flank of a nearby bull.

Bellowing in pain and instinctive animal rage, the steer began to thrash about furiously: bucking as if he was a broncho. His panic quickly spread through the rest of the small herd.

Jason had seen such infectious frenzy before and his eyes widened in anticipation of what he knew was about to follow.

Stampede!

As the cattle began to swarm toward his position, Jason's gaze lit on the bolting horse that had belonged to the second rustler he had killed with his knife.

Knowing he was almost certainly doomed if he remained afoot, the bounty hunter struggled to reach the horse. Dodging horns and hooves with the skill of a matador, he made his way toward the horse.

Reaching the blindly frightened beast, he threw himself up onto its back. Landing in the saddle and snatching at the reins, he saw yet another rider: frantically making his way up the west side of the gully. Mankiller assumed this to be the last of his targets, Rueben Keeler.

He had no time to worry about the Comanchero now, though. His own escape had to be paramount in his thoughts and actions.

Reining his horse around sharply, Jason tried to urge the animal to a gallop. If he could get out ahead of the stampeding cattle long enough to reach the north end of the gully, he would then be able to swiftly tail away and let the herd pass him by.

This plan fell apart when his mount stumbled and nearly fell under him. By the time it righted itself, steers were surging on either side of it.

A large bull slammed against the horse, sliding partly under it. In response, the bovine snapped its head up, hooking the horse's underbelly with one horn. The horn ripped upward in a gory, bloody spray.

The horse reared in pain and fear and pitched to one side: screaming wildly as the raging herd trampled it to death. Thrown from its saddle, Jason hit the ground and began to roll, hoping to reach the relative safety of the sloping wall of the gully.

He nearly made it.

The bounty hunter yelled in raw agony, felt a crushing weight descend on his right forearm as he was stomped on by one of the stampeding steers.

Fighting against the nerve-shocking pain, Mankiller continued to roll until he found himself pressed against the gully's west wall. There he lay face down, arms over his head as the herd continued to stamp by. The taste and smell of their dust filled his mouth and nose, threatening to suffocate him.

So frightened were these stolen steers, he thought, that they might not stop running until they were nearly back to their home grazing grounds.

When at last the terrified beeves had passed and the dust had settled, Mankiller pushed himself up into a sitting position against the slope of the gully. Only now was he able to assess the full damage his right arm had sustained.

His shirtsleeve had been shredded. The odd angle at which the lower arm was now bent spoke volumes. The discoloration and swelling, along with his inability to so much as slightly wiggle his fingers told him that he had as feared suffered a break in his forearm. The potentially fatal consequences of this descended upon him like a falling boulder.

For now…his gun hand was totally useless.

CHAPTER 42

Mankiller's broken arm needed immediate tending—and he was alone.

He figured he could probably just follow the recently liberated cattle back to the 2-B ranch and there receive adequate medical attention: the capability of knitting broken bones was an essentially acquired skill on any such self-sustaining spread.

But doing so would cost him as much as two or three days: plenty of time for the fleeing Rueben Keeler to vanish off the face of the earth.

That option was not acceptable to the tough-minded bounty hunter.

The first thing he had to do was learn if he still had a horse. Holding his right arm against his side with his left hand, he walked back to where he had left the buckskin tethered: sighing gratefully when he found the mount still there.

Again using his left hand, he felt for the wound on his neck: it was sore to the touch but no longer seemed to be bleeding. Wetting a kerchief with water from his canteen, he cleaned the wound: then, as best he could with one hand he tied the kerchief round his throat.

Next came the hard part.

From the trunk of a scrub pine tree he was able to use his knife and good hand to peel loose two wide and relatively straight pieces of wood.

From his saddlebags, he pulled a fresh shirt. He didn't try to don it: rather, using his skinning knife and his teeth, he tore several strips of cloth from it. He dug out another bottle of rotgut whiskey from the same bag.

He scouted about until he found the final object he needed to fill his immediate needs: a short, stout young mesquite tree that had a narrow fork in its trunk just a few feet above ground level.

The drifter dropped down and sat with his back pressed against the mesquite. Uncorking the whiskey bottle with his teeth, he began to take generous gulps of its fiery contents. His eyes watered, and he wondered how anyone such as the old sot he'd plied back in Rio Caballo could ever learn to stomach such brew: let alone consume it in such quantities as to become addicted to its liquid charms.

Still, he forced himself to continue taking deep pulls of the liquor. By the time the bottle was half empty, he was unquestionably under its effects: but not so far under as to have lost control of his faculties. He was ready now to take the next, most difficult step.

Standing and facing the mesquite, he used his left hand to gingerly raise his right arm and firmly wedge its wrist into the fork of the tree's trunk.

After taking another swallow of the rotgut, he began to slowly but firmly pull back on his broken arm as hard as he could bear.

His teeth clamped together, stifling most of a groan. Sweat broke out along his hairline and began to flow down his face. His stomach clenched, threatening to spill its contents from the pain.

So intense were the electrical sparks shooting up his arm and into his body that he feared the very real possibility of blacking out: but he refused to allow that to happen.

Blocking out any thoughts but those of success, he continued pulling back from the mesquite. He didn't stop, but rather intensified his efforts when he at last began to feel and hear the grinding sound of the broken halves of his forearm scraping against each other.

The awkward bend in his arm began to straighten, even as the agony this produced rose to a level few men could have borne to inflict upon themselves.

After what seemed like hours of torture, he was rewarded with a loud snap as the two broken halves of the bone popped roughly back into place: fitting back together more or less as nature intended.

Still struggling to remain conscious, panting heavily, Mankiller again used his good hand, his teeth and the strips of cloth he had prepared beforehand to tie the flat pieces of pine wood to his set right arm. Doing so resulted in the making and applying of a crude but effective splint to hold the bones of his forearm in place so the break could begin to heal.

Once he finally succeeded in tying the makeshift splint sufficiently securely, he sat against the tree and took another long draw on the whiskey bottle.

Then he allowed himself to pass out.

When he regained consciousness two hours later, Mankiller's first action was to fling the nearly empty liquor bottle as far away from him as he could.

His broken arm was still throbbing with pain, but not so much as before he had set it. Normal color and feeling had mostly returned to his right hand: he found he could now move its fingers slightly. He was forced to admit, though, that it would be of little use to him for some time to come.

Now would be the time to put to the test the hours of exercising he had done to train his left hand to function nearly as well.

If he could survive what lay ahead, he might seek the services of a real doctor to have a better job done of setting his injured arm: but for now what he had done on his own would suffice.

Still woozy from the effects of pain and booze, he knew his need for real sleep and restoration of his strength was more critical than ever. The drifter found a more sheltered spot for himself and his horse and commanded himself to sleep. Such were his prodigious recuperative powers that he awakened naturally before first light.

His growling stomach forcefully reminded him that he had also not eaten a real meal in two days. With no immediate need to conceal his location, he allowed himself the luxury of a fire: using it to brew a small pot of coffee and to cook a generous portion of bacon and beans.

He then made preparation to hunt down Rueben Keeler.

CHAPTER 43

First, Mankiller removed his gunbelt. Extracting all the bullets from their belt loops, he shoved them into his left pants pocket.

The .44 Colt revolver he slipped into his pants' belt in such a way that he could pull it out in a cross draw with his left hand. The empty holster and gunbelt he stowed in one of his saddlebags.

Mounting the buckskin horse, he awkwardly withdrew his Henry repeating rifle from its scabbard on the right side of the saddle.

Using his left hand, he attempted to cock the lever on the weapon by simply spinning the rifle with the one hand. The effort didn't go well, with the lever only ratcheting halfway and the rifle nearly flying out of his hand.

He was far more adept with his left hand than were most right-handers, and had put in a great deal of practice learning to smoothly handle and accurately fire a pistol with it. But this move was new and foreign to him. To be even close to effective, he needed to find another way to cock the Henry properly.

He could still bend his otherwise useless right arm at the elbow and cradled the barrel of the rifle in its crook. This held it just securely enough to enable him to then work the gun's lever with his left hand and jack a round into the chamber.

The drifter gently lowered the hammer back down: now all he needed to do in order to fire the gun was pull the hammer back and squeeze the trigger. He didn't return the rifle to its scabbard: instead balancing it in front of him, on the saddle. He then put the heels to his horse.

Finding a spot as close as possible to where he recalled having seen Keeler fleeing during the stampede, Jason moved along the sloped wall of the gully until he cut the trail of a single set of horse tracks leading up and out of the wide depression.

From the rim of the gully, the tracks led due west. Scanning the horizon, Mankiller saw that if the Comanchero didn't deviate from that path he would eventually ride directly into a short range of small mountain peaks.

"Yah!" he urged the buckskin, sending it off in pursuit of his prey. He kept the horse at a trot that ate up miles at a good clip, so as to narrow the several-hour's long lead Keeler had on him. Yet he held it down to a pace still slow enough for the man to keep his eyes on the tracks, while not wearing down the buckskin.

A few hours later, he came upon the remnants of a campfire. He dismounted, letting the buckskin blow and graze while he squatted to study the signs at the scene. Crushed blades of long grass that had not yet fully sprung back up showed Keeler too had taken time to sleep.

Perhaps, Jason surmised, the Comanchero assumed he was safe once he escaped the gully and the herd of stampeding cattle. That theory seemed to be confirmed when the bounty hunter checked the tracks leading away from the campsite. The hoof prints were closer together now than they had been before the outlaw made camp: indicating that when he left the site his horse was walking rather than running.

If Mankiller had his way—the Comanchero's carelessness would prove to be the death of him.

Taking a knee, the bounty hunter cautiously poked a finger into the ashes that were all that remained of the outlaw's campfire. They were nearly cold, but still retained a very mild residual heat.

After removing his kerchief from his neck, he moistened it anew and used it to wipe down the buckskin's head and neck: then gave the animal a welcomed drink of water he had poured into his hat. Only then did the man take time to sit on the ground and eat a strip or two of jerky.

Once he figured he and the horse to be sufficiently rested, the drifter swung back into the saddle and set the buckskin back to its ground-chewing, trotting pace.

Every bounding step the horse took sent a slight stab of discomfort through Jason's splinted arm, which he lessened slightly by riding with it held a bit away from his body.

Within a couple of hours, the bounty hunter had closed the distance between him and the fleeing outlaw enough to spy horse droppings so fresh as to still glisten with moisture.

But this also led him to rein in his mount slightly: slowing enough to diminish the likelihood of rushing headlong into a trap or ambush.

Neither materialized: and as he reached the base of the first of the small range of mountains his heart quickened as he at last saw the object of this manhunt.

Keeler and his horse were slowly picking their way up the slope: along what barely deserved to be called a trail. The horse was clearly struggling to make its way up the narrow, steep incline and was no more than two hundred yards above and beyond where Mankiller sat watching.

Jason dismounted and securely tethered the buckskin, then moved to take up position behind a boulder. He laid the barrel of his rifle atop the rock to steady it before taking a bead on the Comanchero.

Holding his breath, he tripped the trigger.

"Dammit!" he cursed as he saw a bloody spout gush from just behind the right shoulder of Keeler's horse. Mankiller had missed his intended target.

He watched in dismay as the mortally wounded horse reared up on its hind legs before pitching over backwards: taking its rider with it.

Jason began frantically trying to lever a fresh round into the chamber of his Henry. By the time he was able to do so, using his awkward technique, and again aim the rifle up the slope of the mountain—he found he had no readily seen target for a shot.

All he could see was the body of Keeler's horse: it had flipped, rolled and slid nearly halfway back down the mountain trail. Its somewhat grotesque, unmoving position told Jason that the animal was dead.

With the object of his pursuit now on foot, possibly injured, Mankiller decided to leave his own mount where it was tethered. He now chose to abandon his rifle as well, returning it to its scabbard before beginning to ascend the precarious trail on foot: trying to carry the gun with him would have left even his one good hand useless for climbing.

The last thing he did before setting out was to use the bottom of his shirt, pulled up and hooked on a high button, to form a simple sort of sling for his broken right arm. This would give it support, keep it still and out of the way, and less prone to further injury.

Well above him on the mountain, Rueben Keeler watched Mankiller from hiding. He had managed to jump free from his tumbling mount, sustaining only minor abrasions in the process.

He grinned wolfishly as the man tracking him rose toward him and could be seen more clearly. Keeler wished he had his rifle: it would take only one fairly easy shot to pick off his pursuer. But the long gun was still in its scabbard, attached to his doomed horse's saddle. The Comanchero figured he couldn't reach it without exposing himself to a clear shot from below.

But any trepidation his predicament might have caused him vanished when he was finally able to see that the man trailing him—whose face he couldn't yet make out because of distance and the hat he was wearing— seemed to be working with only one arm. And the left arm at that: most likely not his good one.

Keeler felt more confident now. He had initially fled on the night of the stampede because the gunfire he heard start it had led him to fear that he and his gang may have been chased down and attacked by half the crew of the 2-B ranch. When he saw no sign of being immediately followed, he had slowed down his flight: while periodically checking his back trail.

Now that he saw pursuit apparently consisted of but a single man, and that one partly crippled, he relaxed.

Mankiller was taking his time climbing upward, with good reason. The trail he was following now was in truth little more than a narrow cut through the rocks. So steep that a mountain goat would have had trouble assaying it, it necessitated him practically crawling as he moved up it. So horizontal was it that Keeler's poor horse might well have plummeted from it even if it hadn't been shot.

The bounty hunter had to be especially sure of his footing with every step given that, should he slip and start to fall, he had only one good hand with which to catch himself. And because he needed that hand to climb, he had to keep his pistol in his belt rather than out and ready for action.

He at last reached the spot where Keeper's horse had expired, pausing there to get a second wind and scan the trail above his position. With the dead animal wedged into the trail and blocking it, Jason had no recourse save to climb over the body.

Partway over it, the body shifted beneath him: threatening to break loose and fall: carrying the bounty hunter with it.

He lay motionless atop it until it stopped its movement, then continued onward. If it was possible, he grew even more alert now: knowing he was probably only a short distance from his prey.

That was proven true when he heard a skittering of rocks from no more than fifty feet above him.

He realized seconds later that the noise was caused by a small landslide—hurtling down the narrow trail and headed straight for him!

CHAPTER 44

With nowhere to go and nothing to provide protective shelter for him, Mankiller's eyes cast about and his mind raced ahead as a cascade of rocks rained down toward him.

At the last possible instant, he reached out to grab a narrow outcropping and swung his body off the trail.

This left him suspended in space, held up by nothing but the strength in his left hand. He ducked his head as the shower of rocks flashed past.

One stone bounded sideways, striking him in the temple. It was a glancing blow, but nearly enough to dislodge him.

He was certain that had he still been on the trail the landslide would have hurled him off the mountainside and to a crushing death. He coughed and closed his eyes as a cloud of swirling dust followed in the wake of the falling rocks.

Hanging on now by little more than the tips of his fingers, and those weakening fast, he frantically dug at the rock with his feet. By luck and nothing else, the toe of one boot finally found purchase, lodging in a thin crack in the stone face of the mountain. He pushed upward, regaining a stronger grip with his hand.

With the last of the dislodged stones finally bounding past him, he swung himself back onto the rock-strewn trail. Feeling certain the landslide had been deliberately started by his prey, he peered upward for any further sign of ambush while also using the time to catch his breath.

Not far above, realizing his attempt to kill the man on his tail had failed, Rueben Keeler pulled back into the rocks to hide and lay in wait for the right opportunity to spring another attack on his persistent pursuer.

Steadying himself with his good hand, pushing up with his feet, Jason continued his ascent. He grew more cautious still when he saw that the trail he was following would lead him to a narrow, flat ledge before continuing on its upward slant.

He remained still, all of him below the eyes out of sight from above, while casting his gaze about for any indication that Keeler was close at hand before committing himself to exposure by crossing the ledge.

There being no such sign, he finally pushed himself up to the ledge and onto his feet. He didn't draw his pistol, but rested his hand on its butt as he set out toward the point where he would have to resume climbing vertically.

Mankiller was within two steps of reaching that position when his ears detected a very faint scraping sound—from behind him.

Without a second's pause or hesitation, he simultaneously crouched, pulled the revolver from his belt and swiveled to the left.

Keeler, who had stepped from his place of concealment fully expecting to have an easy target with his back turned, was now caught flat-footed.

This was it: the exact moment when all the many hours spent training himself to become nearly ambidextrous could pay off royally for Mankiller. Or could leave him at the mercy of his foe.

While not as fast and fluid as when using his dominant hand, a left-handed Jason Mankiller proved still to be better at his deadly craft than most any other man was.

Keeler got a shot off first, but because Jason had dropped down as he spun, the Comanchero's bullet sailed over his head, ricocheting harmlessly off the mountain's unyielding stone face.

Keeler was not so lucky. Mankiller's shot struck the outlaw low on his right side: spinning Keeler partly around and knocking his feet out from under him.

As the Comanchero struck the ground, his gun flew out of his hand. Grimacing in pain, he nonetheless struggled to crawl forward, striving to retrieve his weapon.

As his trembling hand reached out for it, though, Mankiller's booted foot kicked up hard enough to send it skittering away and over the rim of the ledge.

His only hope gone, Keeler lay flat on the ground for a moment, then slowly pushed himself up to his knees. He slapped his hand over the spot on his right side where the bullet had struck him, hoping to staunch the flow of blood.

The outlaw raised his head, and only now did he clearly see the face of the man who had hunted him down. His eyes widened in surprise as he recognized that face and its teardrop tattoo.

"I can't believe yer still alive," he moaned.

"No thanks to you, Keeler," the drifter said. "You knew damned good and well what waited for me when you gave me over to the Comanches."

"Then how the hell did you get away from 'em?"

"The only way possible," Jason told him. "By being even tougher 'n' meaner than they are."

Looking at the Comanchero's upturned face, Mankiller saw that he had unintentionally spoken truly on that earlier occasion when he had taunted the outlaw about having had his left eye plucked from his head.

In falling and scrambling about, Keeler had lost his covering patch. Jason could see now that it had not merely covered an eye gone sightless.

There was no eye there at all: only an ugly, puckered little crater where the orb had been before something or someone had torn it from its socket. He also noted that the hand Keeler held over his seeping wound was missing its little finger.

Keeler squeezed his remaining eye shut as a pain shot through his belly. When he opened it again, he shook his head.

"I don't get it," he said. "After managing ta get away with yer scalp intact—why risk yer life tracking me down?"

"Not just you, Keeler. You're just the last. Chavez and the breed have already gone to their reward."

"So this was payback fer what we done to ya."

"Partly. But I also mean for it to send a message."

"What sorta message?" the Comanchero asked, clearly confused. "Ta who?"

"To everyone," Jason replied. "When the story of what I've done spreads—and I'll make sure that it spreads—trust me, the message will be heard loud and clear.

"You may be able to defy God and the Devil and get away with it. But anyone who tries to take on the Man Who Cries Blood will pay dearly for the privilege."

Keeler chuckled humorlessly at this. "Well, I guess you made yer point, hardcase. I'm yer prisoner." He raised both arms up before him, fists clenched and wrists pressed together.

"Prisoner?" Mankiller repeated coldly, raising his pistol and cocking the hammer ominously.

"Mister…what makes you think I mean to take you in *alive*?"

THE END

AFTERWORD

The extermination of the buffalo and the ultimate military defeat and destruction of the once mighty Comanche Nation also virtually eliminated the livelihood of those men known as Comancheros.

The Texas Rangers, disbanded after the Civil War, were re-commissioned as a peacekeeping force in 1874. Their efforts put a final end to the depredations of such outcasts.

Nor did the Indian tribes of the Comancheria fare much better.

In response to the Comanches' attack on Adobe Walls, Secretary of War W.W. Belknap instructed General William Tecumseh Sherman to "punish" all hostile Indians in the region.

Sherman, in turn, ordered General Philip Sheridan to "make every Kiowa and Comanche knuckle down."

He drove his point home deeply and sharply by reminding Sheridan that: "The more Indians we kill this year, the less will have to be killed the next."

In response to these orders, in the fall of 1874 General Sheridan dispatched five columns of   soldiers, 3,000 men in all, into the Texas Panhandle.

They converged from five different directions in a classic pincer movement that brought them into direct and repeated conflict with the Comanches and their Kiowa allies.

What followed was a series of more than a dozen minor battles that collectively came to be known as *The Red River War.*

Relatively few casualties were inflicted by either side: but among those who fell fatally in combat was Jason Mankiller's Kiowa "brother," Three Pony—who thus fulfilled his vow never to become a farmer.

Most significantly, each battle further diminished the Indians' supplies of and access to shelter, horses and food.

As autumn progressed, and faced with a winter of deprivation and starvation, most of the remaining Kiowa and Comanche bands sued for peace.

By the middle of 1875, the last of the Comanche holdouts—the fierce Quahadis—surrendered: leaving their cherished Staked Plains for life on a reservation near Fort Sill in the Indian Territory.

Decades later, at the dawn of the 20th Century, one of the early silent moving pictures to be made was a short film entitled *The Bank Robbery.*

It was produced and shot in 1908 in the town of Cache, in the new state of Oklahoma, by the Oklahoma Mutoscope Company.

The plot of the film was simple. After outlaws rob the bank of Cache, a posse forms and tracks them down to their hideout in the Wichita Mountains. A gunfight ensues, in which all the outlaws are killed or captured. The stolen loot is returned to the bank and the surviving robbers are thrown in jail,

One of the "actors" playing a member of that film posse...was the 62-year-old Comanche chief, Quanah Parker.

-THE END-

ABOUT OUR CREATORS

AUTHOR –

R. A. Jones is a native of Oklahoma (originally Indian Territory) where he still resides. R. A. has been a freelance writer and editor for the past thirty years.

His credits include newspaper and magazine columns, articles and short stories. He has been a movie reviewer and commentator in newspapers and on radio. He assisted actor Gary Lockwood (Star Trek; 2001: A Space Odyssey) in the writing of Lockwood's autobiography, *2001 Memories: An Actor's Odyssey*. With Michael Vance, R. A. co-wrote the syndicated comic book and comic strip review column *Suspended Animation* for five years.

The readers of *Comic Buyer's Guide* magazine voted him "Favorite Writer About Comics" in 1985, and in 2006 he was inducted into the Oklahoma Cartoonists Collection Hall of Fame.

He has scripted more than 100 different issues of various comic book titles in his career. Among the more noteworthy are Wolverine and Captain America for Marvel Comics; *Harlan Ellison's Dream Corridor* for Dark Horse Comics; and Star Trek: Deep Space Nine for Malibu Comics. He also co-wrote, for Image Comics, *Bulletproof Monk*, which served as the basis for the 2003 movie of the same title.

His comic book stories, "Cold Hard Facts" and "Three On A Match" which originally appeared in the magazine *Metal Hurlant*, were short films in France.

His novels include *Deathwalker*, *Global Star* (written with Michael Vance and Mel Fox), *The Equation* (co-written with Michael Vance), *The Steel Ring*, a superhero book based on characters from one of the earliest publishers of comic books, Centaur. He also wrote the Western thriller, *Gun Glory*.

INTERIOR ILLUSTRATOR –

CHRIS KOHLER - Comics, and the creation of such, have been an obsession for most of my life. Many years had been spent trying to be the next John Byrne (or at least, the next Sal Buscema…) while floundering for some sort of direction and style to go along with the passion. Several more years were spent doing everything *but* drawing.

Finally, at age 30, there was a synergy between the discipline required in order to draw and the joy felt due to drawing. Since then, a couple hundred pages of comics or so have been born between short stories for small press groups such as Hidden Agenda Press and Approbation Comics, and commissioned pieces done via eBay and deviant Art.

From 2009-2013, I worked with writer Daniel VanderMolen on my largest work to date (over 80 pages), a zombie strip called *Portland Underground* (www.pdxunderground.net). Another couple of years were spent creating 32 pages of EC-style shorts with writer Larry King (no relation!), to be published, at a later date, under the title of '*Tales of Woe*'.

In addition to small press & web comic work, I've been doing interior illustrations for New Pulp publications such as Van Plexico's entire *Sentinels* novel series (8 books so far), and a couple of one-off collections such as *Blackthorn* and *The Many Worlds of Ulysses King*.

COVER ARTIST –

ADAM BENET SHAW –Accomplished painter, illustrator, and comics creator, Adam has garnered acclaim across a number of artistic media. After completing studies at the Cleveland Institute of Art in Ohio, the Edinburgh College of Art in Scotland and Watts Atelier in California, Shaw was selected as an emerging American artist to watch by European gallery owners and exhibited in London, England.

Adam has been featured in "New American Painting", selected multiple times for the Arkansas Art Center's Delta Exhibit, and shown at the prestigious "Red Clay Survey" at the Huntsville Museum of Art. His work has also been shown in over 50 group and solo shows in the US and internationally. His figurative paintings are a prominent part of a 140-foot mural entitled "The History of Cotton" at the National Cotton Exchange Museum, St. Jude's Children's Research Hospital, the National Contact Bridge Museum, and a treasured part of private and corporate collections.

Adam has created storyboards for several motion pictures, including Paramount Pictures' film "Black Snake Moan" directed by Craig Brewer, stage design for operas and corporate events, and character illustrations for the gaming industry. His published graphic novel work includes the series "Dead In Memphis", "Bloodstream" for Image Comics, "David: The

Illustrated Novel" from Shepherd King Publishing and "Harpe: America's First Serial Killers" from Cave-in-Rock Publishing. He shares his love of art through teaching and workshops at his studio in the Broad Avenue Arts District in Memphis. Recently he has been painting book covers for pulp publishers Pro Se Productions and Airship 27 Productions.

Where the story started:

HIS NAME WAS MANKILLER

Young Jason Mankiller never believed his surname was an omen of his future until the Civil War broke out and he joined the Union Army. Fate took him to the fields of Gettysburg. By the time the battle ended, he was sitting atop a small rise surrounded by the bodies of dozens of Confederate troopers. Days later, while drunk, his fellow soldiers had tears of blood tattooed onto his face. From that day forward, the Man Who Cried Blood's reputation spread far and wide.

Ten years later, Jason Mankiller is in Ft. Rogers, Texas, hoping to find a job and bury his past. But the blood tattoo won't let him escape the gunfighter's trail. Writer R.A. Jones delivers an old fashioned western adventure in the grand tradition of Max Brand and Louis L'Amour. Here are pioneering men and women facing the birth of a new American destiny that will demand their blood, sweat, tears and sacrifice. For Jason Mankiller, that promise of a better life will be claimed at the end of a smoking gun.

GUN GLORY

HE RODE A GUNFIGHTER'S TRAIL

R.A. Jones

AN AIRSHIP 27 PRODUCTION

AIRSHIP27HANGAR.COM

NEW PULP

PULP FICTION FOR A NEW GENERATION!

FOR AVAILABILITY: AIRSHIP27HANGAR.COM

More from this author:

BOUNTY ON A KILLER

MOTOR CITY MANHUNT

It's 1935 in Detroit, the city is in the midst of a heat wave when a beautiful white woman is brutally raped and murdered, setting off a powder keg. The chief suspect is a recently paroled black man. Fearing for his life, he goes into hiding only to discover that the victim's father, a rich retired judge, has put a bounty on his head; one million dollars for his apprehension; *dead*.

Standing between the fugitive and a lynching mob are detectives Michael Yellowstone, an Osage Indian, and his partner, Lt. Jack Hill. Yellowstone is determined to find King and bring him in alive. What he doesn't know is that Hill has a totally different goal in mind.

Writers Michael Vance and R.A. Jones offer up a tense, suspenseful thriller that explodes across the pages wherein money hungry citizens are transformed into blood thirsty hunters in the biggest manhunt of them all.

R.A. JONES · MICHAEL VANCE

AN AIRSHIP 27 PRODUCTION

AIRSHIP27HANGAR.COM

NEW PULP

PULP FICTION FOR A NEW GENERATION!

FOR AVAILABILITY: AIRSHIP27HANGAR.COM

www.ingramcontent.com/pod-product-compliance
Lightning Source LLC
Chambersburg PA
CBHW051126260626
47170CB00005B/1687